PENGUIN BOOKS

WHEN THE GREEN WOODS LAUGH

H.E. Bates was born in 1905 at Rushden in Northamptonshire and was educated at Kettering Grammar School. He worked as a journalist and clerk on a local newspaper before publishing his first book, *The Two Sisters*, when he was twenty. In the next fifteen years he acquired a distinguished reputation for his stories about English country life. During the Second World War, he was a Squadron Leader in the R.A.F. and some of his stories of service life, *The Greatest People in the World* (1942), *How Sleep the Brave* (1943) and *The Face of England* (1953) were written under the pseudonym of 'Flying Officer X'. His subsequent novels of Burma, *The Purple Plain* and *The Jacaranda Tree*, and of India, *The Scarlet Sword*, stemmed directly or indirectly from his war experience in the Eastern theatre of war.

In 1958 his writing took a new direction with the appearance of *The Darling Buds of May*, the first of the popular Larkin family novels, which was followed by *A Breath of French Air*, *When the Green Woods Laugh* and *Oh! To be in England* (1963). His autobiography appeared in three volumes, *The Vanished World* (1969), *The Blossoming World* (1971) and *The World in Ripeness* (1972). His last works included the novel *The Triple Echo* (1971) and a collection of short stories, *The Song of the Wren* (1972). Perhaps one of his most famous works of fiction is the best-selling novel *Fair Stood the Wind for France* (1944). H.E. Bates also wrote miscellaneous works on gardening, essays on country life, several plays including *The Day of Glory* (1945); *The Modern Short Story* (1941) and a story for children, *The White Admiral* (1968). His works have been translated into 16 languages and a posthumous collection of his stories, *The Yellow Meads of Asphodel*, appeared in 1976.

H.E. Bates was awarded the C.B.E. in 1973 and died in January 1974. He was married in 1931 and had four children.

H. E. BATES

When the Green Woods Laugh

PENGUIN BOOKS

in association with Michael Joseph

Penguin Books Ltd, Harmondsworth, Middlesex, England
Penguin Books, 625 Madison Avenue, New York, New York 10022, U.S.A.
Penguin Books Australia Ltd, Ringwood, Victoria, Australia
Penguin Books Canada Ltd, 2801 John Street, Markham, Ontario, Canada L3R 1B4
Penguin Books (N.Z.) Ltd, 182–190 Wairau Road, Auckland 10, New Zealand

—

First published by Michael Joseph 1960
Published in Penguin Books 1963
Reprinted 1967, 1972, 1974, 1975, 1978

—

—

Made and printed in Great Britain
by Richard Clay (The Chaucer Press) Ltd,
Bungay, Suffolk
Set in Monotype Bembo

When the green woods laugh with the voice
    of joy,
And the dimpling stream runs laughing by;
When the air does laugh with our merry
    wit,
And the green hill laughs with the noise
    of it:

BLAKE: *Songs of Innocence*

1

AFTER parking the Rolls Royce between the pig sties and the muck heap where twenty young turkeys were lazily scratching in the hot mid-morning air Pop Larkin, looking spruce and perky in a biscuit-coloured summer suit, paused to look back across his beloved little valley.

The landscape, though so familiar to him, presented a strange sight. Half way up the far slope, in fiercely brilliant sunlight, two strawberry fields were on fire. Little cocks-combs of orange flame were running before a light breeze, consuming yellow alleys of straw. Behind them the fields spread black, smoking slowly with low blue clouds that drifted away to spread across parched meadows all as yellow as the straw itself after months without rain.

'Burning the strawberry fields off,' Pop told Ma as he went into the kitchen. 'That's a new one all right. Never seen that before. Wonder what the idea of that is?'

'Everything'll burn off soon if we don't get rain,' Ma said. 'Me included. As I said to the gentleman who was here this morning.'

Ma was wearing the lightest of sleeveless dresses, sky-blue with a low loose neckline. Her pinafore, tied at the waist, was bright yellow. The dress was almost trans-parent too, so that Pop could see her pink shoulder-straps showing through, a fact that excited him so much that he gave one of her bare olive-skinned arms a long smooth caress, quite forgetting at the same time to ask what gentle-man she was referring to.

'Why I'm cooking on a morning like this I can't think,' Ma said. Her hands were white with flour. Trays of apricot flans, raspberry tarts, and maids-of-honour covered the kitchen table. A smell of roasting lamb rose from the stove. 'I'd be watering my zinnias if I had any sense. Or sitting under a tree somewhere.'

Pop picked up a still warm maid-of-honour and was about to slip it into his mouth when he changed his mind and decided to kiss Ma instead. Ma returned the kiss with instant generosity, her hands touching his face and her mouth partly open and soft, making Pop think hopefully that she might be in one of her primrose-and-bluebell moods. This made him begin to caress the nape of her neck, one of the places where she was most sensitive, but she stopped him by saying:

'You'd better not get yourself worked up. That gentleman'll be back here any minute now. Said he'd be back by half past eleven.'

'What gentleman?'

'This gentleman I told you about. He was here just after ten. Said he wanted to see you urgently.'

Insurance feller, Pop thought. Or fire extinguishers. Something of that breed.

'What'd he look like?'

'Dark suit and a bowler hat and a gold watch-chain,' Ma said. 'And in a big black Rolls. With a chauffeur.'

'Sounds like a brewer,' Pop said, laughing, and started to take off his biscuit-coloured summer jacket. Thinking at the same time that a glass of beer would be a nice idea, he paused to ask Ma if she would like one too.

'Had two already this morning,' Ma said. 'Could face another one though.'

Pop put the maid-of-honour in his mouth and started to move towards the fridge. Ma, who was rolling out broad fresh flannels of dough, looked up suddenly from the pastry board as he came back with two iced bottles of Dragon's Blood and laughed loudly, her enormous bust bouncing.

'You look a fine sketch,' she said. 'Better go and look at yourself in the glass before your visitor arrives.'

Pop, looking into the kitchen mirror, laughed too, seeing his face covered with flour dust where Ma had kissed him.

'Good mind to keep it on,' he said. 'Might frighten this feller away.'

He was, he thought, in no state for visitors; it was far too hot. He also had it in mind to ask Ma if she was in the mood to lie down for a bit after lunch. Mariette and Charley were at market; the rest of the children wouldn't be home till four. There wouldn't be a soul to disturb the peace of the afternoon except little Oscar.

'Well, you'd better make up your mind one way or the other quick,' Ma said, 'because here comes the Rolls now.'

Pop sank his Dragon's Blood quickly and Ma said: 'Better let me get it off,' and lifted the edge of her pinafore to his face, wiping flour dust away. This brought her body near to him again and he seized the chance to whisper warmly:

'Ma, what about a bit of a lie-down after lunch?' He playfully nipped the soft flesh of her thigh. 'Feel like it? Perfick opportunity.'

'Don't get me all excited,' Ma said. 'I won't know where to stop.'

In a mood of turmoil, thinking of nothing but how pleasant it was on hot summer afternoons to lie on the bed with Ma, Pop reluctantly walked into the yard. It was so hot that even the turkeys had given up scratching and were now gathered into a panting brood under an elderberry tree from which black limp inside-out umbrellas of berries were hanging lifelessly. Over in the strawberry fields lines of flame were still darting and running about the smoking straw and from the road the sound of the Rolls Royce door snapping shut was as sharp as a revolver shot in the sun-charged air.

It was in Pop's mind to dismiss whoever was coming with a light-hearted quip such as 'Not today thank you. Shut the gate,' when he stopped in abrupt surprise.

Ma's visiting gentleman in the dark suit, bowler hat, and gold watch-chain had suddenly turned out to be a woman in a white silk suit covered with the thinnest of perpendicular black pencil-lines and with a small black and white hat to match.

She came across the yard, plumpish, blonde, chalky pink about the face and pretty in a half-simpering rosebud sort of way, with outstretched hands.

'Mrs Jerebohm,' she said. 'How do you do?' She spoke with the slightest of lisps, half laughing. 'You must be Larkin?'

Pop, resenting the absence of what he called a handle to his name no less than the intrusion on his plan for a little privacy with Ma, murmured something about *that* was what he always had been and what could he do for her?

Lisping again, Mrs Jerebohm said, with a hint of rapture:

'Mr Jerebohm simply couldn't wait to see the house for himself. So that's where he's gone and he wants us to meet him there. I hope that dove-tails all right? You know, fits in?' It was not long before Pop was to discover that dove-tailing was one of Mrs Jerebohm's favourite and most repeated expressions. She simply adored things to dove-tail. She simply loved to have things zip-up, buttonhole, click, and otherwise be clipped into neat and unimpeachable order.

'If we like it I hope we'll have it all zipped-up this afternoon,' she said. 'That's the way Mr Jerebohm likes to do business.'

Silent, Pop feigned a sort of ample innocence. What the ruddy hell, he asked himself, was the woman talking about?

'They told us at the inn you wanted to sell and the minute we heard we had a sort of thing about it.'

Inn? Pop could only presume she meant The Hare and Hounds and at the same time couldn't think what that simple pub had to do with her constant lisping raptures. She fixed him now with eyes as blue as forget-me-nots and a quick open smile that showed that two of her front teeth were crossed. That explained the lisping.

'Could we go right away? I mean does that dove-tail and all that? We could go in the Rolls.'

Pop, bemusedly thinking of roast lamb and mint sauce, cold beer, fresh apricot flan, and Ma lying on the bed in nothing but her slip or even less, suddenly felt a spasm of impatience and used the very same expression he had once used to Mr Charlton, in the days when he had been as eager as a hunter to collect taxes.

'You must have come to the wrong house, Madam,' he said. 'Or else I'm off my rocker.'

'Oh! no.' When Mrs Jerebohm flung up her hands with a rapturous lilt, which she did quite often, it had the effect of stretching the white suit across her bust, so that it momentarily seemed to puff up, tightly. It made her, Pop thought, with her smallish blue eyes and crossed teeth, not at all unlike a white eager budgerigar.

'Oh! no,' she said again. 'That doesn't fit. There can't be two people who own Gore Court, can there?'

It had hardly occurred to Pop, quick as ever in reaction, what she was talking about before she fluttered lispingly on:

'You can show us over, can't you? You do want to sell, don't you?'

'Going to pull the whole shoot down one of these days,' Pop said, 'when I get the time.'

Mrs Jerebohm expressed sudden shock with prayerful lifts of her hands, bringing them together just under her chin.

'Oh! but that's awful sacrilege, isn't it? Isn't that awful sacrilege?'

Pop started to say that he didn't know about that but the first words were hardly framed before she went lisping on:

'But we could just see it, perhaps, couldn't we? At the inn they assured us you were keen to sell. You see we're mad to have a place in the country. Absolutely mad. So when we heard –'

'Big place,' Pop said. 'Fifteen bedrooms.'

'That would suit us. That would fit all right. We'd want to have people down. My husband wants shooting parties and all that sort of thing.'

'Ah! he shoots does he?'

'Not yet,' she said, 'but he's going to learn.'

A sharp, searching fragrance of roast lamb drifted across the yard, causing Pop to sniff with uplifted nostrils. Ma, he thought, must be opening the oven door, and with relish he also remembered maids-of-honour, raspberry tarts, and apricot flans. He wondered too how many vegetables Ma was cooking and said:

'Couldn't manage nothing just now, I'm afraid. My dinner's on the table.'

'Oh? Not really?'

'Ma'll be dishing up in ten minutes and she won't have it spoiled.'

'Oh! be an angel.'

The appeal of the small forget-me-not eyes was too direct to resist and Pop answered it with a liquid look of his own, gazing at Mrs Jerebohm with a smoothness that most women would have found irresistibly disturbing. It was like a slow indirect caress.

On Mrs Jerebohm it had the effect of making her retreat a little. She seemed to become momentarily cool. She showed her crossed teeth in an unsmiling gap, much as if she had realized that her fluttering 'Oh! be an angel' had gone too far into realms of familiarity.

'I can wait for you to finish your lunch,' she said. 'I'm perfectly content to wait.'

'Oh! come in and have a bite,' Pop said. 'Ma'll be pleased to death.'

Mrs Jerebohm gave an answer of such incredible frigidity that Pop almost felt himself frozen in the hot July sunshine.

'No thank you. We never eat at midday.'

Pop could find no possible answer to this astounding, un-real statement; it struck him as being nothing but a fabulous lunacy. It couldn't possibly be that there were people who didn't eat at midday. It couldn't possibly be.

'I will wait in the car.'

'Have a wet then. Have a glass o' beer,' Pop said, his voice almost desperate. He was feeling an urgent need for a glass, perhaps two, himself. 'Come and sit down in the cool.'

Mrs Jerebohm, already cool enough as she surveyed the piles of junk lying everywhere across the sun-blistered yard, the now prostrate brood of turkeys and the Rolls Royce incongruously parked by the muck-heap, merely showed her small crossed teeth again and said:

'Have your dinner, Larkin. I'll be waiting for you.'

Turning abruptly, she went away on short almost prancing steps towards the road. Instinctively Pop gazed for a moment at the retreating figure in its pencilled white skirt. The hips, he thought, were over-large for the rest of the body. As they swung fleshily from side to side they looked in some way haughty and seemed frigidly to ad-monish him.

Going back into the house he felt something more than thirst to be the strongest of his reactions. The morning had suddenly become unreal. In a half-dream he poured him-self a glass of beer, drank part of it and then decided he needed a real blinder of a pick-me-up to restore his sanity.

Ma was busy laying the lunch table as he concocted a powerful mixture of gin, whisky, and French vermouth, a liberal dash of bitters and plenty of ice.

'Been gone a long time,' Ma said. 'What did he want after all?'

In a low ruminative voice Pop explained to Ma that his visitor was, after all, a she.

'Wants to buy Gore Court. Wants me to show her and her husband over after dinner.'

'What's she like? No wonder you been gone a long time.'

Pop swirled ice round and round in his glass, moodily gazing at it. He drank deeply of gin, whisky, and vermouth, waited for it to reach his empty stomach and then in tones of complete unreality revealed to Ma the shocking news that he had just met someone who, believe it or not, never ate at midday.

'Can't be right in her mind,' Ma said.

'Fact,' Pop said. 'Invited her in to lunch but that's what she said. Never eats at midday.'

'Why? Does she think it common or something?'

Pop said that could be it and drank solidly again. A moment later Ma opened the oven door and took out a sizzling brown leg of lamb surrounded by golden braised potatoes, so that the morning at once woke into new excruciating life, with pangs of hunger leaping through Pop like a pain.

'You hear something new every day,' he said, 'don't you, Ma? Something as shakes you.'

Ma said you certainly did and then suddenly, with no warning at all, popped the leg of lamb back into the oven again.

'You mean she's still waiting out there? She'll faint off or something.'

More than likely, Pop thought. Yes, she was waiting. Depressedly he poured another couple of inches of gin into his glass, hardly hearing Ma say:

'I'd better take her a bite of something out. Glass of milk and a slice of flan or something. She can't sit out there on an empty stomach. She'll go over.'

Less than a minute later Ma was away across the yard on an errand that was less of mercy than one of sheer correction. It simply wasn't right for people to do these things. It was as plain as the moon: if you didn't eat you didn't live. It was criminal. You faded away.

Pop had hardly mixed himself a third pick-me-up before Ma was back again, bearing the offering of apricot flan and milk, now rejected.

'On a very strict diet,' Ma said. 'Trying to get her weight down. Got a proper chart and pills and units and points and all that sort of thing.'

Pop, remembering Mrs Jerebohm's over-rounded thighs, tight in the thin white suit, was suddenly jolted by piercing shrieks from Ma. Her great sixteen-stone body seemed to be laughing from every pore.

'I told her to look at me,' Ma said. 'I think it cheered her up a bit. She was no more than a sylph, I said.'

Pop put the word away in his mind for further reference. Ma took the sizzling leg of lamb from the oven again and a few moments later Pop was deftly carving it into generous pink-brown slices, to which Ma added steaming hillocks of fresh-buttered French beans, two sorts of potatoes, new and braised, mint sauce, and vegetable marrow baked with cheese.

Bent over this feast in attentive reverence, Pop at last

paused to drain a glass of beer and look up at Ma and say:

'Ma, what did I pay for Gore Court in the end? I forget now.'

'First it was going to be nine thousand. Then it was seven.'

Pop helped himself to five or six more new potatoes, remarking at the same time how good they were in the long hot summer, and then sat in thought for a moment or so.

'What shall I ask? Ten?'

'Show a nice profit. Might be able to have that swimming pool Mariette keeps talking about if you brought the deal off.'

There was a lot of land there, Pop reminded her. And all those greenhouses and stables and asparagus beds. To say nothing of the lake and the cherry orchard. He thought he'd ask twelve.

'Why not fourteen?' Ma said serenely. 'You can always come down.'

Pop said that was true, but was Ma quite sure it wasn't too much?

'Not on your nelly. Look at the paltry bits of land they ask five hundred for nowadays. Don't give it away.'

No chance of that, Pop said. Not if he knew it. No fear.

'Go up a bit if anything,' Ma said. 'No harm in trying. Ask fifteen.'

Pop, ruminating briefly, thought he detected sense in this and finally, with an airy flourish of a hand, said he thought it wouldn't choke him if he asked seventeen.

'Now you're talking,' Ma said. 'Now you're using your loaf.' She laughed suddenly, in her rich, quivering fashion.

'Might be able to have the swimming pool heated now. You know how I hate cold water.'

Less than half an hour later, after eating three slices of flan, half a dozen maids-of-honour, and a raspberry tart or two, at the same time abandoning with reluctance the idea of a nice lie-down with Ma, Pop put on his light summer jacket again and went out to Mrs Jerebohm, leaving Ma at the task of feeding little Oscar, now eighteen months old, with much the same lunch he and Ma had had themselves, except that it was all mashed up and in smaller proportion. Oscar, he proudly noted, was getting as fat as a butter ball.

Out in the road a chauffeur in bottle green cap and uniform held open the door of Mrs Jerebohm's Rolls and Pop stepped into an interior of beige-gold, the upholstery softer than velvet.

'Well, here we are,' Pop said. 'Perfick afternoon.'

'I see you too have a Rolls,' Mrs Jerebohm said.

'Oh! that old crate. That's a laugh.'

Pop, who in reality adored and revered the Rolls with pride and tenderness as if it had been the eighth of his off-spring, cheerfully proceeded to tear the car's paltry reputation to pieces.

'Took it for a small debt,' he explained. 'Wouldn't pull pussy. Knocks like a cracked teapot. You'd get more out of a mule and a milk float. Still, the best I can afford. Struggle to make ends meet as it is.'

As the Rolls turned the last bend before the house faded from sight he invited Mrs Jerebohm to look back on his pitiful junk-yard, the paradise from which he scratched the barest of livings – if he had good luck.

'Like my poor old place,' he said. 'Just about had it.

Falling apart and I'll never get the time to put it together again.'

'Charming countryside, though,' Mrs Jerebohm said. 'I adore the countryside.'

Pop resisted a powerful impulse to praise the country-side. Nothing in his life, except Ma, brought him nearer to celestial ecstasies than the countryside. Instead he now started to concentrate, with a new warm glow, on fresh enthusiasms.

'Ah! but wait till you see Gore Court. Wait till you see that.'

'I'm absolutely dying to. Absolutely dying. We've seen so many that haven't – you know – sort of dove-tailed, but this one gives me a kind of thing –'

A moment later Mrs Jerebohm took a handkerchief from her white suède handbag, releasing an unrecognizable breath of perfume on which Pop's hypersensitive nostrils at once seized with eager delight.

It was a wonderful perfume she was wearing, he said. Could she tell him what it was?

'Verbena. French. You like it?'

It was perfick, Pop said. It suited her perfickly. It was just her style.

'Thank you.'

She smiled as she spoke, this time with her lips parted a little more, so that the edges of her mouth were crinkled. The effect of this was so surprisingly pleasant after the frigidities in the yard that Pop wondered for a moment whether or not to hold her hand and then decided against it. Even so, he thought, it might not be all that much of a hardship to dove-tail with Mrs Jerebohm one fine day.

He was still pondering on the pleasant implications contained in the word dove-tail when the Rolls rounded a bend by a copse of sweet-chestnut, beyond which were suddenly revealed a mass of baronial turrets taller than the dark torches of surrounding pines.

'There!' Pop said. He spoke with a studied air of triumph, waving a hand. 'There's the house. There's Gore Court for you. What about that, eh? How's that strike you? Better than St Paul's, ain't it, better than St Paul's?'

2

MR JEREBOHM, who had stayed the night with Mrs Jerebohm at The Hare and Hounds, had been up that morning with the lark. He was not at all sure what sort of bird a lark was or what it looked like, but he knew very well it was the bird you had to be up with.

Numbers of small brown birds in the many thick trees surrounding the pub, which both he and Mrs Jerebohm called the inn, had chirped him awake as early as half past four. He supposed these might have been larks. On the other hand they might well have been robins. He was a stranger in the country; it was a foreign land to him, distant as Bolivia, unfamiliar as Siam. He simply didn't know. Nor did he know anything distinctive about the trees which stood about the pub with tall lushness, almost black in high summer leaf. A tree was a shape. It had branches, a trunk, and leaves. In spring the leaves appeared; they were green; and in autumn they fell off again.

Grass was to be recognized because it too was green, or generally so. It grew on the floor, most conveniently, and cows grazed at it. Mr Jerebohm recognized a cow. It had horns, teats, and gave milk. If it didn't it was a bull. He also recognized a horse because even in London, where stockbroking absorbed him day and night, you sometimes still saw one drawing a cart. You also saw them on films and television, running races. You also hunted foxes with them, which was what Mr Jerebohm hoped to do as soon as he and Mrs Jerebohm had finally settled on a suitable place in the country.

Finding a suitable place in the country had turned out to be an unexpectedly difficult and tedious business. The notion that you rang up or called on a house-agent, described the kind of residence you wanted – Mr Jerebohm invariably referred to houses as residences and their surroundings as domains – and bought it immediately was nothing but a myth. This was not in the least surprising, since myths were exactly what house-agents dealt in. They were crooks and liars. Their sole idea was to sell you pups.

Mr Jerebohm was determined not to be sold any pups. Nobody sold him any pups in the world of stockbroking and nobody was going to sell him any in the world of larks and cows. He was, since he was a Londoner, clever enough not to be caught by that sort of thing. People in London were naturally clever. They had to be; it was due to the competition.

On the other hand, everybody knew that people in the country were not clever, simply because there was no need to be. There were enough fields, trees, cows, horses, and all the rest of it to go round. You had ample milk, fresh from the cow. You kept hens and they laid multitudes of eggs. Farmers made butter. As to the people, you smelled innocence in the air. They were naturally simple. The sky, even when rainy, was full of purity. The fields had a sort of ample pastoral virginity about them, unbesmirched by anything, and even the manure heaps had a clean, simple tang that was good to breathe.

The exceptions to all this were house-agents. Two weeks of trailing with Mrs Jerebohm from one to another had made Mr Jerebohm tired and angry. He was now constantly taking pills and powders for the suppression of bouts of dyspepsia brought on by viewing manor-houses which turned out to be matchboxes, farms which were nothing but hen-coops and country residences of character which looked like disused workhouses or mental homes.

He wanted no more of house-agents at any price and for this reason had been more than glad when the barman at The Hare and Hounds had told him that a fellow named Larkin had a very nice house that he was planning to pull down. It was a pity and a shame, the barman said, but there it was. Nobody seemed to want it.

'You're sure it's nice?' Mr Jerebohm said. He had heard that word about houses before; it was the most misused, the most callous, in the language. 'Has it class is what I mean?'

Class was what Mr Jerebohm was looking for and class was precisely what couldn't be found.

'I ought to know,' the barman said. 'My missus goes in to air it twice a week and cleans and dusts it once a fortnight. You could walk in tomorrow. Class? – it's a treat. All in apple-pie order.'

Mr Jerebohm thanked the barman and gave him a shilling. It paid to be generous to the yokels.

'Pinkie,' he said that night as he folded his charcoal city trousers and hung them on the bedroom towel-rail, 'Pinkie, I've got a sort of hunch about this house. A funny kind of premonition. Have you?'

Pinkie was his pet name for Mrs Jerebohm; it suited her much better than Phyllis.

Pinkie, who in nothing but panties and brassière was squatting on her haunches in the middle of the bedroom floor, hands on hips, balancing a Bible and a thick telephone directory on her head, going through her slimming exercises, said she thought so too, adding:

'I think I've lost another ounce. I weighed myself today in the ladies' at that hotel where we had lunch. But I can't really tell until we get home and I can take everything off and get on the proper scales.'

Mr Jerebohm, saying good for her, got into bed, propped himself up on the pillows and started to read the *Financial Times*. The night was exceptionally hot and stuffy and in any case he knew from long experience that there was no need yet awhile to think of shutting his eyes. It would take Pinkie the best part of another hour to do her balancing acts with books, stretch her legs, touch her toes, do press-ups, take off her make-up and swallow her pills.

'Good night, Sunbeam,' she said when she got into bed at last. She liked to call him Sunbeam last thing at night; it left a blessed sort of glow in the air. 'Sleep well.' She kissed him lightly on the forehead, barely brushing his skin, anxious about her facial cream. 'I'm mad to see this house. It's so beautiful here. Don't you think it's beautiful?'

Mr Jerebohm wasn't sure whether it was beautiful or not. Hot and restless, he found he couldn't sleep well. It was terribly noisy everywhere. The countryside not only seemed to be full of barking dogs. From the fields came a constant moaning of cattle and whenever he was on the verge of dropping off he was assailed from all sides by low asthmatic bleatings.

Later in the night he had a rough bad dream in which Pinkie lost so much weight that she became a skeleton and he woke in an unpleasant sweat to hear a whole eerie chain of birds hooting at each other from tree to tree. These, he supposed, might well have been owls, though he wouldn't have been at all surprised to hear that they were nightingales.

Whatever they were they kept him awake until dawn, when once again the larks started their maddening chorus in the ivy.

3

W HEN Pop Larkin first saw Mr Jerebohm, hatless and coatless in the heat, waiting outside the tall wrought-iron gates by Gore Court, it struck him immediately that his face seemed in some way curiously out of proportion with the rest of his body.

Mr Jerebohm was shortish, squat, and slightly paunchy beneath watch-chain and waistcoat. By contrast his face was rather long. It was greyish in an unhealthy sort of way, with thick loose lips and eyebrows that had in them bright sparks of ginger. He looked, Pop told himself, rather like a bloater on the stale side.

'Afternoon, afternoon,' Pop said. 'Perfick wevver. Hope I haven't kept you waiting? Hope you don't find it too hot?'

Mr Jerebohm, who in sizzling heat had tramped about the domain of Gore Court for the better part of an hour, so that his dark city trousers were now dustily snowy with white darts of seed from thistle and willow-herb, confessed to a slight feeling of weariness. But Pop was cheery:

'Cooler inside the house. Wonderfully cool house, this. Thick walls. I daresay,' he said, 'it's above twenty degrees cooler inside. Had a good wander round?'

Mr Jerebohm confessed that he had wandered but wasn't sure how good it was. He had learned to be craftily cautious about houses. He was going to be very wary. He wasn't going to be sucked in.

'Had to fight my way through a damn forest of weeds,'

he said. 'Look at me. How long has the place been in this state of disrepair?'

Pop laughed resoundingly.

'That seed?' he said. 'Blow away in a night. One good west wind and a drop o' rain and it'll melt away. Put up any pheasants?'

When Mr Jerebohm rather depressingly confessed that he hadn't put up a bird of any kind, Pop laughed and said:

'Hiding up in the hot wevver. Place's crawling wiv 'em. Partridges too. And snipe. And woodcock, down by the river. Didn't see the river? I'll take you down there when you had a deck at the house. And the lake? Beautiful trout in the lake. Nice perch too. Didn't see the lake? Didn't get that far? I'll take you down.'

Mrs Jerebohm, following Pop and Mr Jerebohm up the circular stone steps leading to the front of the house from a short avenue of box trees, found herself borne along on a mystical flow of lilting information that might have come from a canary. It was so bright and bewildering that she was inside the house before she knew it, standing at the foot of a great baronial sweep of oaken stairs.

'There's a flight of stairs for you,' Pop said. He waved a demonstratively careless hand. 'Handsome, eh? Like it?'

Mrs Jerebohm, almost in a whisper, went so far as to say that she adored it. If anything clicked, that staircase did.

Cautious as ever by contrast, Mr Jerebohm struck the banisters of the stairs a severe blow with the flat of his hand, as if hoping they would fall down. When nothing happened Pop startled him with a sentence so sharp that it sounded like a rebuke:

'Built like a rock! – wouldn't fall down in a thousand years!'

With hardly a pause for breath Pop enthusiastically invited Mrs Jerebohm to take a good deck at the panelling that went with the stairs. It was linen-fold. Magnificent stuff. Class. There were walls of it. Acres. Talk about fumed oak. Fumed oak wasn't thought of when that was made. You could get ten pounds a square foot for it where it stood. And that was giving it away. And did she see the top of the stairs? The Tudor rose? The Tudor rose was everywhere.

Mrs Jerebohm, speechless, stood partly mesmerized. At the very top of the stairs, lighting a broad panelled landing, a high window set with a design of fleur-de-lis, swans, and bulrushes in stained glass of half a dozen colours threw down such leaves of brilliant light, driven by the strong afternoon sun, that she was temporarily dazzled and had to pick her way from step to step, like a child, in her ascent of the stairs.

A man from Birmingham had offered him a thousand pounds for the window alone, she heard Pop say in a voice that reached her as an unreal echo, like some line from a far distant over-romantic opera, but he had turned it down.

'Class,' Mr Jerebohm was half-admitting to himself. 'Class.'

'How old is the house?' Mrs Jerebohm brought herself to say. Her voice too was like an echo.

Pop said he thought it was Georgian or Tudor or something. Fifteenth century.

Mr Jerebohm, with bloater-like smile, was quick to seize on these transparent contradictions and nudged Pinkie quietly at the elbow as they turned the bend of the stairs. It served to prove his point about how simple the yokels were.

'How many bedrooms did you say?' Mrs Jerebohm unable to keep entrancement out of her voice, almost hiccupped as she framed the question. 'Was it ten?'

Twelve, Pop thought. Might be fifteen. If it was too many they could always shut the top floor away.

'There's a beauty of a room for you!' he said with almost a bark of delight. A huge double door, crowned by a vast oaken pediment, was thrown open to reveal a bedroom half as large as a tennis court. 'Ain't that a beauty? Didn't I tell you it was like St Paul's?'

Mrs Jerebohm, stupefied by sheer size and acreage of panelling, heard three pairs of footsteps echo about her as if in a cave. Above them, at the same time, the chirpy solo voice of Pop was urging her to take a good eyeful of the view from a vast blue and pink window that might have come out of an abbey.

'Drink that in!' he said. 'Take a swig at that!'

Mrs Jerebohm, in half-ecstatic rumination, found herself positively gulping at two acres of thistles, willowherb and docks among which numbers of black conical cypresses and a half-derelict pergola of roses stuck up in the air like a sad fleet wrecked and abandoned. Beyond them a line of turkey oaks, black too in the blistering perpendicular light of full afternoon, cut off completely whatever view was lurking behind.

'In winter,' Pop started to say with a new, more vibrant lyricism, 'in winter, when the leaves are down, and the light's right, and it's a clear day, in winter, Mrs Jerebohm, you can stand here and see the sea.'

In a rush of disbelief, lyrical too, Mrs Jerebohm several times repeated the words in heavy lisps.

'The sea? – the sea? No? Really? The sea?' she said. 'You mean we can really see the sea?'

'Smoke of ships in the channel,' Pop said impassively, 'coming from all over the world.'

'Oh! Sunbeam,' Mrs Jerebohm said, lisping, 'you hear that? You can actually see ships out there. Ships!'

Mr Jerebohm, impressed though still wary, had no time to make any sort of comment before Pop struck him a resounding but friendly blow in the middle of the back. Mr Jerebohm recoiled uneasily but Pop, totally unaffected, merely told him:

'This is the place where you got to use your loaf, old man. Get your imagination to work. Have a deck down there.'

As Pop waved a careless hand in a quick flexible curve in the direction of the impossible thistles Mr Jerebohm half ducked, as if confident of another approaching blow, but Pop merely urged him, taking a great deep breath:

'Imagine roses down there. Imagine acres of roses. Eh? A couple o' thousand roses.'

Without another word he suddenly flung open a casement in the church-like window, again drawing a long deep breath.

'What price that air, eh? Take a sniff at that. Like medicine. Old man, that's pure concentrated iodine.'

'Iodine?' Mr Jerebohm, incredulous, snapped sharp, bloater-like lips. 'Iodine? What on earth's iodine got to do with it?'

With stiff wariness Mr Jerebohm waited for an answer.

determined not to be caught by any cock-and-bull non-sense of that sort.

'Air here's stiff with it,' Pop said. 'Saturated. Due to being practically surrounded by sea.'

To the speechless astonishment of both Mr Jerebohm and Pinkie he proceeded to toss off careless scraps of topo-graphy.

'Got to remember this country is almost an island. Didn't know that? Fact. Two-thirds of its boundaries are water. It's an island on an island. Understand me?'

Before Mr Jerebohm could begin to say whether he understood him or not Pop thundered out:

'Nobody hardly ever dies here. People live for ever, same as tortoises. Everything grows 'ell for leather. Cherries, strawberries, hops, apples, pears, corn, sheep. Everything! Not called the Garden of England for nothing, this place. Not called the Garden of England for nothing, old man.'

Suddenly, after Pop had closed the casement with a gesture almost dramatically regretful, Mrs Jerebohm felt quite overpowered, in a faint sort of way, by the projected grandeur of sea-scape, roses, iodine, and heights, and asked diffidently if perhaps she could see the kitchens?

'Certainly!' Promptly Pop started to lead the way downstairs, freely admitting as he did so that the kitchens were perhaps a bit on the large side, though of course that wasn't necessarily a bad thing these days. It gave you a lot more room to put telly in for the maids.

That, Mrs Jerebohm said, reminded her of something. Help. What about help? Could help be got? In London that, of course, was the great problem. Would she be able to get help in the country?

'Sacks of it,' Pop said. 'Bags.' If his conscience pricked him slightly as he recalled the constant eager race of village women to get to the rich pastures of strawberry fields, cherry orchards, and hop gardens and all the rest, where families cleaned up sixty or seventy pounds a week, tax free, he momentarily appeased it by reminding himself that, after all, business was business. A fib or two was legitimate. You had to allow for a fib or two here and there. 'All the help you want. Only a question of paying on the right scale and giving 'em plenty o' telly.'

Lispingly Mrs Jerebohm confessed that she was relieved to hear it. The question had been bothering her. It was the thing on which everything depended.

'Quite,' Pop said blandly. 'Quite.'

A moment later he opened the door to the kitchens. A vast funereal dungeon opened up, half-dark, its windows overgrown with rampant elderberry trees. The air was drugged with mould.

'Something would have to be done with this,' Mr Jerebohm said. 'Not much iodine here.'

Pop, severely ignoring the sarcasm about iodine, freely admitted once again that it was all a bit on the large side but anyway you could always put in a ping-pong table for the maids. Help 'em to keep their figures down. He laughed resoundingly. They got fat and lazy quick enough as it was.

Mr Jerebohm, in turn ignoring the joke, started to retreat with relief from the dankness of the kitchen dungeons, saying:

'You're quite sure about the help? What about chaps for the garden and that sort of thing?'

'Oceans of 'em,' Pop said. 'No trouble at all.'

His conscience, pricking him slightly a second time, forced him to think of farm labourers who ran about in cars or mounted on splendid, glistening, highly expensive motor-bikes and of how his friend the Brigadier couldn't get a boy to clean his shoes, and he wondered, not for the first time, what Ma would say. Ma was strict about the truth. Still, you'd got to allow a fib or two here and there.

'Well, I hope you're right.' Mr Jerebohm told himself he wasn't sold yet. Much experience with house-agents, the liars, cheats, and swindlers, had left him sceptical, cautious, and, as he liked to tell himself, sharp as a fox. 'It's of paramount importance.'

Pop, recoiling slightly from the word paramount as if it meant something shifty, said:

'Well, now, what else?' He too was relieved to escape from the kitchens' dank elder-mould darknesses and he was bound to admit they ponged a bit. 'What about a look at the outside?'

He searched the air for a breath of Mrs Jerebohm's light and exquisite perfume and, as he caught it, made her smile with perceptible pleasure by saying:

'That scent of Mrs Jerebohm's reminds me of Ma's garden. She grows verbena there.'

'You see, we'd plan to do a fair amount of entertaining,' Mr Jerebohm said. 'That's why I spoke about the chaps. Shooting parties and that sort of thing. Lot of people at week-ends.'

'Beautiful shooting country,' Pop said. 'Marvellous. Bags of cover. What about a look at the lake now?'

Mr Jerebohm said yes, he was ready to have a look at the lake if Pinkie was.

'You go,' she said. 'I'd like to wander round the house again.'

As she started to go upstairs Pop, in the moment before departing, called up after her:

'If you change your mind it's straight down from the front of the house. You'll see the path. There's a white gate at the bottom.'

As he skirted the seed-smoking thistle forest with Mr Jerebohm Pop put to him what he thought to be an important question:

'What business you in?'

'Stock Exchange.'

'Plenty o' work?'

'Mustn't grumble.'

'Hot weather affected you at all?' Pop said. 'It's caned a lot of people.'

'Not really.' Mr Jerebohm couldn't help smiling behind his hand. Really the yokels were pretty simple. And when you thought of it how could they be otherwise?

'There's the lake for you,' Pop said. 'Beautiful water-lilies, eh? Always remind me of fried eggs floating about on plates.' The lake, low after months of drought, stretched glassy in the sun. On banks of grey cracked mud flies buzzed in thick black-blue swarms. An odd invisible moorhen or two croaked among fringes of cane-dry reed and out on the central depths great spreads of water-lilies shone motionless in the sun.

Pop picked up a stone, aimed it at a distant clump of reeds and threw it. It might have been a signal. A line of wild duck got up, circled, and headed for the centre of the lake, crying brokenly as they flew.

'Thought so,' Pop said. 'Whole place is lousy with 'em.'

Pheasants? Mr Jerebohm supposed.

'Wild duck.' Dammit, these Londoners were pretty simple when you came to think of it. 'Like wild duck? Ma does 'em with orange sauce. Puts a glass o' red wine in too. I love 'em. Shot so many last winter though I got a bit sick of 'em by the end.'

For a painful moment or two Mr Jerebohm's sharply watering mouth told him he would never, never get tired of wild duck. He longed suddenly and passionately for wild duck with red wine and orange sauce, tired as he was of living on Yoghurt, toast fingers, consommé, and undressed salads in order to help Pinkie keep her weight down.

'And all this goes with the house? The lake and everything?' he said. 'What's beyond?'

'Parkland. See the big cedar?'

Mr Jerebohm stared at a tall dark object on the skyline and might as well have been looking at a factory chimney. 'Starts there. Quite a few deer in it still. Used to be a pretty big herd. Like venison?'

God! Mr Jerebohm thought. Venison?

'Ma always does it in a big slow double pan in plenty of butter,' Pop said. 'Nothing else, just fresh butter. We always have red currant jelly with it. The meat fair falls apart. Perfick. I tell you, old man, perfick.'

Mr Jerebohm, who had lunched exceptionally early, in unison with Pinkie, on thin slices of lean ham, butterless rye biscuits and China tea, thought 'God!' again in agony, feeling his stomach perform involuntary sickening acrobatics of hunger. There was something not fair about talk of food sometimes.

'Not sure how the trout are holding up,' Pop said. He'd got to be fair about the trout. No use over-praising the trout. To be perfickly fair the herons fetched them almost as fast as you re-stocked and you never really knew how they were. 'Caught sight of two or three fat ones though, last time I came down. Still, it's cheap to re-stock if you wanted to.'

Mr Jerebohm, staring hard at the lake as if in hope of seeing a fish rise, resisted with great difficulty a powerful and insidious temptation to ask how Ma dealt with trout.

'Same with pheasants,' Pop said. 'You'd have to start thinking of re-stocking soon if you wanted to shoot this autumn.'

'I thought you said the place was stiff with them?'

'Old birds,' Pop said with swiftness, unperturbed. 'Pretty wild too. You want a couple o' hundred young 'uns. It's not too late. They're well advanced this summer. Hot wevver.'

Mr Jerebohm, deeply tormented again by agonies of hunger, suddenly abandoned all thought of foxiness and dizzily saw himself as the proud master of all he surveyed. The whole scene was simply splendid. This, he thought, was it. Lake, trout, pheasants, park, deer, wild duck, venison – God, he thought, this must be it.

Rapture left him abruptly a moment later, leaving him rational again.

'What, by the way, are you asking?'

'Going to farm?' Pop said.

The question, short and simple though it was, was an astute one. If Mr Jerebohm was going to farm he naturally wanted to lose money. Pop knew most of the dodges and this was the popular one. You made it in the city and lost it on the land. The countryside had never been so full of ragged-trousered brokers – what he called the Piccadilly farmers – pouring their money down the furrows.

'Roughly the idea,' Mr Jerebohm said. 'Pleasure too of course. Mrs J. is mad keen to have a nice rural domain.'

'I've been asking nineteen thousand.'

That ought to dove-tail it all right, Pop thought. Mr Jerebohm, though speechless, didn't flinch. A few thistle seeds, borne on the lightest of winds, floated angel-wise down the bank of the lake, here and there settling on reeds and water. Mr Jerebohm watched them with eyes that might have been idle but were sharp enough to see a fish rise in a startled circle, a moment later, far out among the water-lilies.

'Big 'un there,' Pop said. 'Ever have 'em blue? The trout I mean. We had 'em in France once and Ma got the recipe. You want plenty o' brown butter. You get 'em fair swimming in brown butter and then they're perfick.'

Mr Jerebohm disgorged a low, hungry sigh. He felt he couldn't bear much more of the poetry of eating and wished to God Pinkie would come and help him out a bit. In vain he looked back in the direction of the house and then said, snapping:

'I'll give you twelve.' Sentimentality was out. Absolutely out. You had to be firm from the beginning. The class was there all right but you had to be firm.

Pop laughed in a certain dry, easy fashion.

37

'I think it's about time I went home,' he said. 'Ma'll be wondering where I've got to.'

'Oh? It's a perfectly good offer in my view.'

Pop laughed again, this time more loudly.

'Well, maybe in your view, old man,' he said, 'but that ain't mine, is it?'

Again Mr Jerebohm wished to God Pinkie would come to help him out a bit. There were times when he needed Pinkie.

'To be perfectly honest I really ought to consult my wife about it first and then let you know,' he said. 'I don't want to be precipitate.'

'Should think not an' all,' Pop said, at the same time wondering what the hell precipitate meant. It sounded like something catching.

'Shall we start to walk back?' Mr Jerebohm said. The afternoon was really shatteringly hot. Sweat was pouring off him in uncomfortable streams. Where on earth was Pinkie? 'I could give you word by Monday.'

Monday, Pop said, might be too late. The chap from Birmingham was coming down again to look at the window and another chap was after the panelling. You didn't see linen-fold like that every day. It was worth all of fifteen hundred if it was worth a bob and once these demolition rats got to work you wouldn't see the place for dust.

The expression 'demolition rats' disturbed Mr Jerebohm to the core. It was even worse than venison with red currant jelly and wild duck with orange sauce. God Almighty, where on earth was Pinkie? As he followed Pop up the path he again looked towards the house in vain.

With inexpressible relief he heard Pop say, less than a minute later:

'Ain't that your missus standing up there under the trees?' Pop paused to point to a grassy knoll, a hundred yards away, crowned by a ring of big sweet chestnuts. 'Waving her hand.'

'Waving both hands!'

It was clear, Mr Jerebohm thought, that Pinkie was in a state of some excitement: unless, as was possible, she was trying out some new slimming exercise. Both arms were waving madly above her head, the hands waggling like spiders.

'Sunbeam!' she started to call. 'Sunbeam!'

The excited lisping call dragged Mr Jerebohm up the slope of parched grass to the knoll as if he had been attached to Pinkie by a rope. He felt unutterably glad to see her and wondered, twice and aloud, what it could be that so excited her?

'Probably came across some buried treasure,' Pop said. 'They say Cromwell was here. One of his prisoners escaped from a window in the house –'

Mr Jerebohm, utterly uninterested in Cromwell, half ran forward to meet Pinkie, who lisped liltingly in return:

'Come and see what I've found. You wouldn't guess in a thousand years.'

Pop started to follow Mr Jerebohm and his wife through the chestnut trees. Masses of prematurely fallen blossom, in dry pollened tassels, had fallen from the trees and clouds of pungent yellow dust were raised as Mr and Mrs Jerebohm ran.

'There! I discovered it. I just absolutely ran across it. I

wasn't thinking of a thing and suddenly it sort of conjured itself out of nowhere. It just sort of dove-tailed –'

A kind of pepper box, in white stone, with a domed roof and a marble seat inside, sat with forlorn elegance among the chestnut trees. Black piles of decaying faggots were propped against one side.

'It's a summer house, isn't it? The sort they built in the eighteenth century?' Pinkie said. 'Didn't they call them follies?'

Folly or not, Pop thought, the chap who built this thing was on my side.

'And the view. You must look at the view.'

Turning, Pop had to admit that the view was pretty stunning. It was better than perfick. The lake, sown with water-lilies and framed with long fingers of reed, could now be seen entire, with park and cedars spread out as mature, calm background. It needed only a herd of deer to run lightly across the cloudless blue horizon to set the last romantic seal on it and send Mrs Jerebohm finally and sedately mad.

'Come and sit inside a minute,' Pinkie said to Mr Jerebohm. 'You'll get the full flavour then.'

Though the shady marble struck with ice-cold shock on Mr Jerebohm's seat Pinkie might have been cased in armour for all she noticed the chill on hers.

'Sunbeam, we've absolutely got to have it. What is he asking?'

'Nineteen thousand.'

'Is it an awful, awful lot?'

'I offered him twelve.'

'Would he split do you suppose?'

'I expect so. I could have a stab.'

Mr Jerebohm knew, in his heart, that whether he had a stab or not it really didn't matter. The folly had finally achieved what roses, panelling, iodine, and sea-scape had failed to do. Whatever doubt remained after trout, venison, duck, and pheasant had done their all-tormenting work had gone for ever.

'Try him with fifteen,' Pinkie said. 'We've got to get it laced up somehow. I couldn't bear –'

A sudden dread of colic made Mr Jerebohm rise quickly from the marble seat, his rump half-frozen. It was a positive relief to get out into the hot, stifling air.

'Well, Larkin, my wife and I have talked it over. I'll give you fifteen.'

'Couldn't do it,' Pop said, speaking with great blandness. 'The demolition rats would give me more than that.'

Mrs Jerebohm recoiled from the expression 'demolition rats' as Mr Jerebohm himself had done down by the lakeside. It was an expression so nauseating that she actually had a vision of real rats, live and repulsive, gnawing away the stone and marble of her beloved folly, and she pinched Mr Jerebohm sharply on the arm.

'I'll split the difference,' Mr Jerebohm said.

'Fair enough,' Pop said. 'Seventeen thousand.'

Mr Jerebohm had no time to protest against the neatness of Pop's arithmetic before Mrs Jerebohm lisped:

'Oh! Splendid. Splendid. I'm so glad we've got it all sewn up.'

Sewn up it was, an' all, Pop thought. Ma would be pleased. And Mariette. They could have the swimming pool easy now. And probably even heated

'Well, that's it then, Larkin.' Mr Jerebohm shook Pop not uncordially by the hand. Mrs Jerebohm, smiling with winning, crossed teeth, shook hands too. 'Thank you. I'll tell my solicitors to contact you. Presume you'd like some sort of deposit?'

Wouldn't cause him no pain, Pop said. Couldn't manage cash? he supposed.

Mr Jerebohm said he didn't see why not. There were times when it was better that way. The times being what they were, in fact, it actually suited him.

As the three of them walked back to the house Pop turned to Mrs Jerebohm's tight, white-suited figure and asked if there wasn't perhaps something else she wanted to see? The kitchen garden? The asparagus beds? The greenhouses?

'You could grow some beautiful orchids there.'

Orchids were one touch of poetry too much for Mr Jerebohm, who said rather peremptorily that thanks, there was nothing else they wanted. At the same moment Mrs Jerebohm pointed across the valley, where smoke from the strawberry fields was still drifting across the blue brilliant sky.

'A fire!' she said. 'Isn't that a fire?'

Yes, Pop said, it was a fire and went on to explain how, for the first time in living memory, they were burning off the strawberry fields. The strawberry lark was over for the year. In a couple of weeks harvest would be over too. Everything would be over. It would all be finished months ahead of time, thanks to the marvellous summer, and he offered Pinkie Jerebohm the final crumb of comfort needed to make her day supremely happy.

'The women'll all be coming in from the fields early this year. You'll get all the help you want in the house. Been a perfickly wonderful summer, don't you think, absolutely perfick?'

It certainly had, Mrs Jerebohm said, it certainly had, and with one long ecstatic backward glance at the lake and its lilies she felt her eyes slowly fill with tears of joy.

This, she told herself, was paradise.

That night Pop felt the deal called for a bottle of champagne in bed with Ma and an extra good cigar. As he sat in bed, sipping and puffing and watching Ma brush her hair at the dressing table, he caught pleasant glimpses of her body, vast and soft, under the forget-me-not blue night-gown, thin as gossamer, he had bought her for Christmas.

'Think the kids were pleased about the swimming pool,' he said, 'don't you? I thought the twins would die.'

At the supper table he had been surrounded by children choking with excitement. The twins were half-hysterical. Montgomery, Victoria, and a fast-maturing Primrose – he wasn't sure she wasn't going to be the prettiest of the lot after all – were not much better.

'Didn't think Mariette and Charley sounded all that wild though,' Ma said.

'No?'

'No. After all you promised you'd build 'em a bunga-low with the stuff you pulled out of Gore Court. And here they are still living with us.'

'Stuff's too good for a bungalow. You couldn't do it,' Pop said. 'I'll give Mariette a thousand for her birthday next month. They can start on that.'

Well, that was nice and generous, Ma said, and got into bed to sip champagne, her nightgown giving off strong clouds of heliotrope, her new perfume.

'Thundering hot still,' Pop said.

Still, he thought, they mustn't grumble. Been a pretty fair day on the whole. He hadn't expected to get more than ten or eleven for Gore Court at the best, but thanks largely to Ma he'd done much better. Ma was a sharp one really. By the way, he said to her, what about Mariette? Any sign of any increase and all that?

'Not yet,' Ma said. 'Charley's going to have a test.'

'Test? Good God.'

The subject of a test was so embarrassing that Pop felt both relieved and glad when Ma changed the conversation abruptly and said:

'You didn't really tell me what Mrs Jerebohm was like.'

Ma, as always, was pleasantly curious, even eager, to hear more of Pop's female acquaintances.

'Fairish,' Pop said. 'Uses some funny expressions. Dithers a lot. Says things like dove-tail and zip-up and clock and so on. Excitable.'

Ma looked sharply up at him at the word excitable and said she hoped he hadn't been up to any hanky-pankies of any sort?

'No, no,' Pop said. 'Nothing like that.'

Ma said she was very relieved to hear it. Unabashed, Pop asked why?

'Because they're going to be our nearest neighbours,' Ma said. 'That's why. We'll be having them in for drinks and all that. You want to start off on the right foot, don't you?'

Pop, sipping champagne, said he didn't mean excitable in that way. He meant she got sort of emotional about little things. He recalled the tears he had seen in her eyes at the lakeside. She was all excitable about the joys of country life and all that lark.

'Expect she thinks eggs grow on trees,' Ma said, 'and cream comes out of a tap.'

Well, it wasn't quite so bad as that, Pop said, but it was a damn cert Mr Jerebohm didn't know a duck from a jackdaw. Typical Piccadilly farmer – every pea-pod was going to cost him a bob and every pheasant a tenner.

'Well, if he don't mind,' Ma said.

Oh! he didn't mind, Pop assured her, it was all part of the game. But what a world, wasn't it? What a world when you had to lose a lot of money so as to make more? What a world, eh?

'Certainly is,' Ma said and went on to say that there were times when she thought we were all half crazy. 'Not sure we haven't forgotten what it's all about sometimes.'

Forgotten what all what was about? Pop wanted to know.

'Oh! you know,' Ma said, 'just being here.'

The sudden conscious reminder that he was alive on a hot summer evening full of stars was enough to recall to Pop something he had meant to ask Ma earlier on.

'Had a good mind to ask you to have a lay-down when I got back this afternoon,' he said, 'but you were watering your zinnias.'

'Well, I'm not watering my zinnias now,' she said, 'am I? You never want to spoil a good mind.'

Pop thought that this, like so much that Ma said, made

45

real sense and presently, after getting out of bed and drawing back the curtains and gazing with his own special sort of rapture at the blazing summer stars, got back into a world of chiffon and heliotrope in order to demonstrate to a silently waiting Ma what a good mind he still had.

4

SEVERAL weeks later, about five o'clock on a warm October evening Pop, in his shirt sleeves, was sitting comfortably in a deck chair on the south side of the house, a quart glass of beer at his side, occasionally potting with a shot gun at odd pheasants flying over from the Jerebohm domain to roost in the bluebell wood beyond the yard.

It was just the sort of shooting the doctor ordered. You sat in comfort, with a nice supply of beer at hand, and picked off the birds like one o'clock. Perfick sport. Like fishing for trout with worms, he didn't suppose it was the real and proper sporting thing to do, but at the same time he reckoned it was streets in front of tramping over sodden stubbles on rainy winter afternoons, waiting for birds to be beaten out of copses at ten quid a time. The pheasant tasted no different anyway and he was very glad he'd managed to persuade Mr Jerebohm to buy a couple of hundred young ones at precisely the right time. Well fed on corn, the birds had fattened beautifully in the extraordinary warm autumn weather and were now as tender and tasty, he thought, as young love. Now and then you missed a bird because at the critical moment you had the beer up to your lips, but on the whole he couldn't grumble. He'd bagged a brace already.

It was not often that he was alone about the house, but Ma and the children, together with Charley and little Oscar, were still hard at the strawberry lark. It was the first time in living memory that the strawberry lark had extended into September and October. There were years when a few odd pounds ripened in autumn but now, thanks to the long hot summer that seemed as if it would never end, there were whole fields of them. Splendid fruit was being gathered in tons. The burnt fields of July had been fed by August thunder rains and had woken into sudden blossoming, as deserts do. It was the most remarkable lark he'd ever known. Ma and Charley and the kids had been at it for six weeks, making pots of dough.

In the fading evening light he missed a bird that planed over too low and too fast for him and then, a minute later, found himself without beer. For a few minutes he sat debating with himself whether to fetch another bottle or to give up shooting altogether and was finally saved the necessity of making a decision by the sight of two figures crossing the yard.

The sudden arrival of the Brigadier, who dropped in quite often, left him unsurprised. It was the sight of Angela Snow, silky haired and lovely as ever, wearing the dreamiest of thin summer dresses, a shade deeper than pale sherry, that made him leap up from his chair. He hadn't seen her since that tenderest of holiday farewells in France, a year before.

'Lambkin,' she said. 'Darling. Given me up for dead or lost or as a bad lot or what?'

Pop, kissed first on both cheeks and then with a light flowering brush on the lips, was actually at a loss for words.

'I was waffling into town to buy an evening paper,' said the Brigadier, who did a great deal of walking, not from choice but necessity, since he couldn't afford a motor, 'and

Angela picked me up in the car. Must say I wasn't sorry either. Been damned hot again.'

The word hot set Pop hurrying to the house for drinks, ice and glasses, which he brought out on a tray vividly scrolled in magenta, orange, and scarlet scenes violently depicting Spanish dancers.

'The Brigadier, poor lamb,' Angela said, 'has been crying on my shoulder.'

The Brigadier, angular, thin, and shabby as ever, the elbows of his alpaca actually looking as if gnawed by mice, coughed several times in embarrassment, quite shy.

'Come, come,' he said. 'Now really.'

'Honest to God,' Angela said. 'And I was the great stupid. I hadn't heard about his sister.'

On a morning in April the Brigadier's sister, going up-stairs with a small pile of ironing and suddenly lacking strength to reach the top, had simply sat down on the middle steps and quietly died.

'Nice brace of birds,' the Brigadier said, eager to change the subject. 'Got them in the meadow, I suppose?'

Pop, pouring large whiskies on to hillocks of ice, laughed resoundingly and explained how the birds, flying over from the Jerebohm domain, were on the contrary picked off in comfort, from the deck chair.

'Good God,' the Brigadier said. Shocked, he relapsed after the two words into immediate silence. It was really a bit beyond the pale. By Jove it really was. Even for Larkin.

'And what,' Angela said, 'is the great big hole doing in the garden?' She laughed flutingly, pointing across the

49

garden to where, beyond the flaming yellows and scarlets of Ma's zinnias, a vast earthwork had been thrown up, dry as stone from the heat of summer. 'The grave for the poor wretched birds as they fall?'

'Swimming pool,' Pop explained.

'Good God,' the Brigadier said again. Whisky in hand, he stared incredulously across the garden, prawn-like brows twitching. The apparent vastness of the pool, seemingly half as big as a public bath, shocked him even more than Pop's unsporting habits with pheasants. Coughing, he tried a dry joke of his own. 'Quite sure it's large enough?'

'Got to be big to take Ma,' Pop said.

'Scream,' Angela Snow said. 'And when do you hope to use it?'

'If the wevver's nice, early next spring,' Pop said. 'Going to have it heated.'

The Brigadier did his well-mannered best not to choke over his whisky. Angela Snow laughed in her incomparably musical fashion, on bell-like notes, her pellucid eyes dancing.

'And shall we be invited for a dip?' she said. 'If we're not I shall write you off as a stinker.'

'Course,' Pop said, 'probably have a party to christen it,' and went on to say yes, Ma would have it heated. If it wasn't heated, she said, she'd have to have a mink bathing suit and what about that? The trouble with Ma was that she wasn't all that much of a swimmer and got cold very quickly. She floated mostly and if it was warm she had more fun.

'I heard of a bathing party once,' Angela said, 'where all

the bathing suits melted as soon as the chaps jumped in. How about that?'

Perfick idea, Pop said. He'd have to think about that. Eh, General?

A certain shyness, not shock this time, left the Brigadier speechless again and it seemed to Pop that Angela Snow, laughing no longer, looked at him with a touch of pity. He suddenly felt overwhelmingly sorry for the General himself. He had heard stories of a daily help serving him bread and cold bacon for lunch or leaving him to dine alone on cold pies of sausage meat as hard as rocks. He felt a chill of loneliness in the air and made up his mind to give the General the brace of pheasants when he left. He could knock off some more tomorrow.

'Another snifter?'

The invitation cheered the Brigadier considerably, though not nearly so much as Pop's sudden recollection of a dish Ma had made that morning and of which there was some left in the fridge. It was a sort of open cheese tart decorated with thin strips of anchovy. It was equally delicious hot or cold. He'd go and get it.

'Ma got the recipe from Mademoiselle Dupont, in France, on that holiday last year,' he said on coming back from the house with the tart, which Ma had cooked in a baking tin a foot wide. 'By the way, Angela, did you go again this year?'

Pop cut handsome wedges of tart and proceeded to hand them to the Brigadier and Angela, who said:

'Couldn't, dear boy. Had to stay at home and look after Iris.'

Pop said Oh? he was sorry about that. Ill or something?

'Nothing so simple, darling. Married.'

For crying out gently, Pop said. That was a surprise. He hadn't thought she was the type.

'Nor did she. Not until that party of yours at the Beau Rivage. That altered the outlook. She lost a precious possession there.'

Pop laughed. He must remember to tell Ma that. The Brigadier, by contrast, showed no sign of amusement at all, not because he was shocked again but merely because he wasn't listening. Chewing with almost excruciating relish on the wedge of cheese tart he stood bemused, a man lost. Two sandwiches of crab paste at lunch time hadn't shown much staying power.

'What about staying for supper?' Pop said suddenly. 'I daresay Ma'll find a couple o' brace o' pheasants. I shot ten or a dozen last week. Expect there'll be strawberries and cream too. Ma generally brings back a few pounds from the field.'

The Brigadier, silent still, felt he could have wept. A prick or two of moisture actually pained his eyes, in fact, as he gave a low cough or two and finally said, in tones intended as cryptic but polite in refusal:

'Oh! no, no, Larkin. Really mustn't. Thanks all the same. No, no, no.'

'Oh! you're a sweetie,' Angela Snow said and the Brigadier looked perceptibly startled, as if thinking or even hoping for a moment that the remark was meant for him, 'of course we'll stay. I'm absolutely starving anyway. Aren't you, Arthur?'

The Brigadier himself had never looked more startled than Pop did at the sudden mention of the General's Christian name, which he had never heard before.

'Good,' he said. 'Good. Ma'll be tickled to death. Especially when she hears you're starving.'

The Brigadier, who was always starving, had nothing to say. The light was fading rapidly now. The scarlet and yellow of Ma's zinnias were like burning embers dropped from the heart of the sunset, the quiet air still like summer, the sky unfeathered by cloud, the sweet chestnut leaves hardly touched by a single brush stroke of brown or yellow. Perfick evening, he heard Pop say as he poured yet another whisky and offered another wedge of tart – that touch of anchovy was masterly, the Brigadier thought, it started all your juices up – and then, a moment later, he heard the first laughing voices of the Larkin family coming home from the strawberry field.

Half a minute later he was aware of a young vision crossing the yard in the twilight. The dark head and olive skin of Primrose were exactly like those of her mother. For a few seconds it actually hurt him to look at her, taller by several inches than when he had seen her last, growing rapidly, her bust ripening. She seemed to him like a younger, less vivacious Mariette. The dark eyes were shy, big and serious, even a little melancholy, and suddenly his heart started aching.

It was uplifted a moment or two later by Ma, carrying in her arms a little Oscar looking as fat as a young seal. Boisterous as ever, brown from weeks of sun, she breezily invited the Brigadier to have a strawberry. In the twilight the baskets of lush ripe berries looked almost black.

'Not surprised to see you here, General,' Ma said. 'But Angela too! Going to stay for supper, aren't you?'

'Already fixed,' Pop said. 'Already fixed.'

'Lovely to see you,' Angela said. 'Can't think what's come over this man of yours, though. Been behaving like a curate. Never a caress.'

'Wait till he gets you in the swimming pool,' Ma said and, laughing like a jelly, went away to put the pheasants into the oven and little Oscar into bed.

The appearance of Mr Charlton, looking astonishingly healthy and brown as a chestnut, startled the Brigadier even more than that of Primrose had done. Charley had filled out a lot too. He was big, even muscular.

'Look remarkably fit, young man,' the Brigadier said and Pop could only think, gloomily, that appearances could be pretty deceptive. He'd begun to think there must be very grave defects in Charley. It was all of two months since Charley had had his tests and neither he nor Ma had the foggiest notion what the results were. The worst of it was Mariette looked astonishingly healthy too. It was a bad sign.

A few moments later he was shepherding everyone into the house, himself carrying the drinks tray, when the telephone rang. Soon afterwards Ma appeared at the door and called:

'Mariette says it's Mrs Jerebohm, wanting me. Will you talk to her? If I'm to get Oscar down and the meal cooked I can't stand there nattering half the night.'

'Charley,' Pop said, 'tot out. Give Angela and the Brigadier another snifter,' and went into the house to answer the lisping voice of Mrs Jerebohm, who said:

'We'd like it so awfully much if you and Mrs L. could come to dinner one evening soon. Thought perhaps the 26th might be nice. It's a Monday – awfully awkward day,

I know, but we're down for a long week-end. Hope it dove-tails with your plans? Know you're always terrifically busy.'

Pop, thanking her, said he was pretty sure it would be all right and if it wasn't he'd ring her back very soon. After he had said this there was a long pause from the other end of the line and he said:

'Hullo. Still there?'

Yes, she said, she was still there.

'Thought you'd gone. Nothing the matter?'

No, she said, nothing was the matter. She giggled briefly. It was just his voice.

'Oh? Well, can't help it,' Pop said, laughing too. 'It's just beginning to break, that's all.'

Mrs Jerebohm giggled again, seemingly as nervous as a puppy.

'No, seriously, it sounds so different. Awfully different, actually. One doesn't connect it with you.'

'Ah! well, sorry about that,' Pop said. 'I'll try to do better next time.'

It was the sort of conversation he forgot as quickly as it was made and after going back into the living-room, where the Brigadier already had a third stiff whisky in his hand, he let it go completely from his mind. He would talk to Ma about the dinner later on, probably in bed, over a final snifter.

Wearing a yellow pinafore, Angela Snow floated gaily from kitchen to living-room, helping Mariette to lay the supper table, talking as she did so in high musical overtones. This, she declared, was her idea of fun. The Brigadier, already feeling the third whisky lifting depression from him like a cloud of dark smoke, watched her going to and fro with eyes looking every moment less and less jaded. The juices of his senses had started waking as sharply as those of his mouth had done over anchovy and cheese, so that he began telling himself over and over again that she was a beautiful, beautiful creature.

Soon the delicious unbearable fragrance of roasting pheasant was filling the house. Every few minutes the Brigadier sniffed openly at it like a dog. It seemed as if a long night, a grey mixture of solitude, sandwich lunches, bone-hard apple pies and cold bacon, was at last breaking and passing him by. He hardly noticed the arrival of a fourth and then a fifth whisky and it was from the remotest ends of a waking dream that he heard Pop calling with ebullient cheerfulness to Mr Charlton:

'Shall we have pink tonight, Charley boy? Why not? Get three or four bottles on the ice quick. Ought to go well with the pheasants, I think, don't you?'

'Darling, if that was champagne you were referring to I shall remain faithful to you for ever,' Angela Snow said. 'I adore the pink. It's absolutely me. Quite my favourite tipple.'

The Brigadier might well have wept again except that now, by some miracle, there was nothing to weep for. Had there ever been? He simply couldn't believe there ever had. He was beginning to feel alive again, terrifically alive. Pink champagne? By God, that took him back a thousand aching years. He was again a crazy subaltern on Indian hill-stations, lean and active as a panther: dances and parties everywhere, polo and pig-sticking, affairs with two married women running at the same time, servants everywhere as plentiful as beetles. He was the gay dog having champagne for breakfast, with a certain madness in the air, and nobody giving a damn.

'Glad to see you're perking up, General,' Ma said as she passed him with two deep glass dishes of strawberries, each containing half a dozen pounds. 'Got your glass topped up?'

'Splendid,' the Brigadier said. 'Splendid. Absolutely splendid.'

'Don't spoil your appetite, though, will you?' she said. 'Supper'll only be ten minutes or so.'

The Brigadier found it suddenly impossible to believe how swiftly the evening had gone. The time had whipped along like prairie fire. He took his watch out of his breast pocket and discovered it to be already eight o'clock. Spoil his appetite? He could have eaten horses.

Ma had cooked two brace of pheasants, together with chipolata sausages, thin game chips, potatoes creamed with fresh cream and the first Brussels sprouts with chestnuts. Brimming boats of gravy and bread sauce came to table as Pop started to carve the birds, the breasts of which crumbled under the knife as softly as fresh-baked bread.

'Tot the champagne out, Charley boy,' Pop said. 'And what about you, General? Which part of the bird for you? Leg or bosom?'

The Brigadier immediately confessed to a preference for bosom and a moment later found his eye roving warmly across the table, in the direction of Angela Snow, who met the gaze full-faced and unflushed, though with not quite the elegant composure she always wore. This started his juices flowing again and with a brief peremptory bark he found himself suddenly on his feet, champagne glass waving.

'To our hostess. I give you a blessing, madam. And honour. And glory. And long, long health –'

The unaccustomed extravagance of the Brigadier's words trailed off, unfinished. Everybody rose and drank to Ma. The Brigadier then declared that the pink champagne was terrific and immediately crouched with eager reverence over his plate, the edges of which were only barely visible, a thin embroidered line of white enclosing a whole rich field of game, vegetables, sauce, and gravy.

Somewhere in the middle of a second helping of pheasant he heard Pop recalling his telephone conversation with Mrs Jerebohm.

'Wants us to go to dinner on the 26th,' Pop said. 'I said I thought it was all right.'

'Having staff trouble, I hear,' the Brigadier said.

'Oh?' Ma said. 'The women'll all come back in the winter.'

'Has to do the cooking herself, I understand.'

'Well, that won't hurt her, will it?' Ma said. 'If she likes good food she'll like cooking it. Same as I do.'

'I can only say,' the Brigadier said, gazing solemnly into the winking depths of his glass, 'that if the dinner she gives you is one tenth as delectable as this – no, one thousandth part as delectable – then you will be feeding on manna and the milk of paradise –'

Once again the extravagant words floated away. With them went the piled plates of the first course, carried out by Mariette and Angela Snow, who brought back bowls of strawberries and cream to replace them.

Soon the strawberries lay on the Brigadier's plate like fat fresh red rose-buds, dewed white with sugar. The visionary sherry-coloured figure of Angela Snow came to pour the thickest yellow cream on them, her voluptuous bare forearm brushing his hand. Then as she went away to take her place at the table a sudden spasm of double vision made him see two of her: a pair of tall golden twins of disturbing elegance who actually waved hands at him and said:

'You're doing fine, Brigadier, my sweet. Does my heart good to see you. This afternoon I thought you were for the coal-hole.'

What on earth she meant by the coal-hole he didn't know and cared even less. He only knew he was doing fine. The strawberries were simply magnificent; they came straight from the lap of the gods. Only the gods could send strawberries like that, in October, to be washed down by champagne, and soon he was eating a second dishful, then a third.

'The General's away,' Ma kept saying with cheerful peals of laughter, 'the General's away.'

Then a renewed and stronger bout of double vision made him miscount all the heads at the table. The twins and Victoria were already in bed, leaving eight people eating. But now sometimes he was counting sixteen heads, then eighteen, then twenty, all of them dancing round the table like figures in a chorus. Behind them the television set glimmered a ghastly green and Pop's extravagant glass and chromium cocktail cabinet shimmered up and down like some impossible garish organ at a fair.

It was to these figures that he found himself saying hearty

and newly extravagant farewells just after eleven o'clock, the brace of newly shot pheasants in his hand.

The evening had been great, he kept saying, swinging the pheasants about with grand gestures. Absolutely great. Straight from the gods. He kissed Ma several times on both cheeks and clasped Pop and Charley with tremendous fervour by the hand. After this he kissed both Primrose and Mariette, saying with unaccustomed gravity, followed by a sudden belch, that Ma and Pop were a million times blessed.

'A million times. A million times. Ten million times.'

Still swinging the pheasants, he started to climb into Angela Snow's car and then paused to give several pleasurable barks in final farewell.

'By God, Larkin, I must say you know how to live!' he said. 'I'll say that for you. I'll say you damn well know how to live.'

Once again he started to swing the pheasants madly about his head and Pop treated him to a sudden clout of affectionate farewell plumb in the middle of the back. The gesture pitched him violently forward and through the open door of the car, unlocking fresh barks of laughter, in which Ma and Angela Snow joined ringingly.

'Sleep well, General!' Ma called. 'Sleep well!'

'Sleep be damned!' the Brigadier said. He waved a majestic hand from the car window, splendidly reckless, eyebrows martially bristling. 'Shan't sleep a damn wink all night! Shan't go home till morning!'

Pop said that was the spirit and urged him not to do anything he wouldn't do. The Brigadier yelled 'Bingo!', exclaiming loudly that he wanted to kiss Ma again.

'Must kiss Ma!' he said. 'Got to kiss Ma. Never sleep if I don't kiss Ma.'

Pop again said that this was the stuff and urged Ma to come forward and give the Brigadier a real snorter, one of her specials.

Ma immediately did so, fastening her lips full on the Brigadier's mouth with powerful suction. The Brigadier, half suffocated, made a rapid imaginative ascent skyward, unable to breathe.

Then Angela Snow called: 'Here, what about me? What have I done? What about this little girl?' so that Pop, not quite knowing at once whether it was his services that were being called for or those of the Brigadier, simply decided that it must be his own and proceeded to give Angela Snow three minutes of silent and undivided attention on the other side of the car.

Pop, who didn't believe in doing things at any time by halves, felt quite prepared to prolong things even further, but even Angela Snow thought there were limits and finally struggled out of the embrace gasping for air, as if half-drowned.

'One for the road?' Pop said. 'Come on, one more for the road.'

'One more like that and I shall be away. There'll be absolutely no holding me.'

'I'm away already!' the Brigadier said. By God, he was too. He had never known sensations like it. Not, at any rate, for a long time. He was sailing heavenwards on imaginary clouds of bliss. There was no stopping him.

'Got your pecker up all right now, haven't you?' Ma said. 'Not down in the dumps now, are you?'

Not only was his pecker up, the Brigadier thought. Everything else was.

'Good-bye, darlings,' Angela Snow called at last to the Larkins. 'Farewell, my lambs. Bless you both ten thousand times. And the same number of the sweetest thanks.'

The Brigadier, not quite fully conscious, felt himself being driven away into a night voluptuous with stars, the good-byes still sounding behind him like a peal of bells. Soon afterwards, with a reckless hand, he was grasping Angela Snow somewhere in the region of a smooth upper thigh and to his very great surprise found there was no whisper of protest in answer.

'Must come into the cottage and have a nip of brandy before you go,' he said, 'eh? Let's broach a keg. Bingo?'

'Bingo,' Angela Snow said. 'You have absolutely the sweetest ideas. I'm dying for a nip.'

Angela, still recoiling slightly from the velvet impact of Pop's long-drawn kiss, felt half light-headed herself as she stopped the car at the cottage, got out, and stood for some minutes waiting for the Brigadier to find his latchkey. All the time he was still swinging the pheasants about with careless gestures.

'Got it.' Key in one hand, pheasants in the other, the Brigadier groped gaily to the cottage door. It was a bit tricky here, she heard him explaining as she followed, and heard him trip on a step. 'Got to find the lights. Should be a torch somewhere.'

The door of the little cottage opened straight into the living-room and the Brigadier, unlocking the door, went inside, unsteadily groping.

'Stand still,' he urged her. 'I'll have a light in a couple of jiffs.'

Suddenly he turned and, in the darkness, ran full against her. A powerful recollection of Ma's divinely transcendent kiss bolted through him in such a disturbing wave that a second later he was urgently embracing her.

The sudden force of it made him drop the brace of pheasants and trip. Angela Snow, caught off-guard, tripped too and they both fell over, the Brigadier backwards, across the hearthrug.

Dazed for a moment, he found it impossible to get up. Then he realized, flat on the floor, that he didn't want to get up. He told himself that only a fool would want to get up. The silk of Angela Snow's dress spread across him in a delicious canopy and finally he put up a hand and started touching, then stroking, her bare left shoulder.

It might have been a signal for Angela Snow to get up too but to his delighted surprise she, apparently, didn't want to get up either. This prompted him to start stroking the other shoulder and a second later, in response, he heard her give a series of quiet, thrilling moans.

'Heavenly,' she told him. 'Keep on. Just between the shoulders. That's it. Just there.'

Great God, the Brigadier thought. He stroked rapidly.

'Slower, slower,' she said. 'Slower, please. Round and round. Slowly. That's it. Heavenly.'

A moment later, with sudden abandon, the Brigadier grasped the zip of her dress and pulled it with a single stroke down her back. In response she kissed him full on the mouth, more softly and tenderly than Ma had done but still with the instantaneous effect as of veins of fire lighting up all over his body.

Something about this electrifying sensation made him say, when the kiss was over:

'By Jove, the Larkins know how to do it, don't they? By Jove, they know how.'

'And they're not the only ones.'

The Brigadier, urged on, began to think that nothing could stop him now and presently he was caressing her shoulders again and unhooking the clip of her brassière.

'Round and round,' he heard her murmur. 'That's it. Round and round. Oh! that's heavenly. How did you find my weak spot? And so soon?'

The Brigadier hadn't the faintest notion. He was only aware of the entire evening flowering into madness.

'By Jove, I could lie here all night,' he said. 'I could see the stars out. I don't want to go to bed, do you?'

'Oh! no?' she said. 'Don't you?'

Half way up the stairs the Brigadier, at the end of an evening of revolutionary sensations, none of which he had experienced for a generation, felt yet another one rise up, out of the darkness to greet him.

Without warning five of Pop's whiskies, ten glasses of pink champagne and several large brandies joined their powerful forces. One moment he was grasping at the bare voluptuous shoulders of Angela Snow; the next he was sitting on the stairs, at more or less the same place where his sister had sat herself down and left him in final solitude, and passed out swiftly and quietly, without a sigh.

When he came to himself again he was alone, fully dressed, on the bed. The autumn dawn was just breaking and in the middle of it a huge and spectacular planet was shining, winking white as it rose.

5

A WEEK later Ma was sure the long, hot summer was at an end. The nights and mornings, she said, had begun to strike very parky. The last of the strawberries were finished; there was frost in the air. She had begun to feel very cold across her back in bed of a night, so that she was glad to tuck up closer to Pop, and already by day she was sometimes glad to wear two jumpers, one salmon, one violet, instead of none at all.

'Think I'll slip my mink stole on when we go to the Jerebohms tonight,' she said.

And by eight o'clock, when she got out of the Rolls outside the big oak front door of Gore Court, she was very glad she had. A cold, gusty, leaf-ridden wind was beating in from the west. Twigs of turkey oak and branches of conifer were flying everywhere.

'I'm duck-skin all across my back already,' Ma said. 'You feel it worse after a hot summer. I hope it'll be warm inside.'

Pop, who had taken the precaution of having three Red Bulls laced with double tots of gin before coming out, said he hoped so too and pulled the big brass bell-knob at the side of the front door.

A clanging like that of a muffin bell echoed through the house, very far away, as if at the end of cavernous corridors. For the space of two or three minutes nobody answered it and presently Pop pulled the bell-knob again. By this time rain was spitting in the wind and Ma said she was freezing to death already. Pop said he wasn't all that hot himself but that was how it was with these enormous houses. The servants always lived half a mile away.

A second or two later the big front door was opened by a girl of nineteen or twenty, blue-eyed and very fair, with her hair done up in the shape of a plaited bread roll. She gave Pop and Ma the slightest suspicion of a curtsey and said 'Good evening. To come in please,' in an accent so strong that Pop, fixing her with a gaze like a limpet, told himself she must be froggy.

Inside the huge baronial entrance hall, lit only by a big brass lamp hanging over the head of the stairs, the air struck cold as a vault. It smelled mouldy too, Ma thought, and a bit mousey into the bargain, rather like that hotel they'd stayed at in Brittany.

'No, I'll keep my stole on,' she said to the girl when she offered to take it, 'thank you.'

'*Bitte*,' the girl said and then corrected herself. 'Please.'

Bitter it would be an' all, Ma thought, if you had to live in this place all winter and couldn't get it no warmer than it was now. She'd get pleurisy in no time.

She thought the drawing-room, huge though it was and with all its treacle-brown panelling about as cheerful as a church vestry, seemed a little better. A fire of birch logs a yard long was sulkily smoking – burning was too definite a word for the thick pink mist gushing out of the silvery pile of wood – in a brick fireplace as large as a cow-stall. The heat that came out of it might possibly have warmed a fly, Ma thought, but not a very big one.

'Ah! Larkin.' Mr Jerebohm, with outstretched hand,

advanced from the smoky regions of the fireplace. 'Mrs Larkin.'

Mr Jerebohm, who was wearing a black velvet jacket and a claret-red bow-tie, said of course they both knew Pinkie, who now simpered rather than walked across the drawing-room to lisp 'Good evening' and shake hands. Pinkie was wearing a silk evening dress of an indefinite brown colour, rather like stale milk chocolate. It was sleeveless, off the shoulder and rather low at the bust, so that some inches of a dough-coloured pouchy bosom were revealed.

'It'll be pride that keeps her warm,' Ma thought. 'Nothing else will.'

Pinkie lisped that it was awfully nice to see them and did they know Captain and Mrs Perigo?

Still clinging to him, is she? Ma thought. Thought she'd run off with that feller Fanshawe long ago.

'Evening,' Pop said. 'Think we've met a couple o' times.'

Captain Perigo said 'Really?' in a voice remarkably like the groan of an un-oiled gate, and said he didn't believe they had. In expressing his words his bony jaw, which was much the colour of pumice stone and about as fleshless, unhinged itself with rusty difficulty and then remained emptily open, unable to hinge itself back again.

'Often seen you ride at the point-to-points,' Ma said. 'My daughter Mariette rides a lot there.'

'Really?' Captain Perigo said.

This monosyllabic eagerness of welcome was in direct contrast to Mrs Perigo, who spoke heartily and had eyes like ripe black olives. If Captain Perigo, from continuous association with horses, looked remarkably like an under-nourished hunter himself, Mrs Perigo had all the plushy creaminess of a cow. In tones like those of a deep-blown horn she drawled good evenings, at the same time giving Pop a look of openly inviting greeting, eyes in a deep slow roll.

High society now, Ma thought. There was a certain mannered stiffness in the air quite foreign to her nature and she was glad she'd brought her mink.

'Our summer seems to have left us, don't you think?' Mrs Perigo said. 'Absolutely heavenly. We'll never have another one like it, ever, will we? I mean ever? You been away?'

'Not this year,' Ma said. 'Been too busy strawberry-picking.'

'Really?' Captain Perigo stared at Ma in open-mouthed pain, as if she had been doing time.

The unmistakable chill in the air prompted Pop to think that a large snifter would go down well. A moment later he found himself confronted with a tray held by Mr Jerebohm. On it were three or four pink glasses, each about the size of a thimble.

'Care for sherry?'

Pop thanked Mr Jerebohm, raised a thimble of pale amber liquid and stared at it dubiously, not certain whether to knock it back in one go or husband it for a while. He decided on husbandry. Something told him there might not be another.

'Admiring your mink,' Mrs Jerebohm said to Ma, who was also holding a thimble. 'Hope you don't mind? Quite gorgeous. That lovely new colour.'

'Bought it with the money I made in the strawberry field,' Ma said. 'Put in a lot of extra time this year.'

Pop, overhearing this, was ready to laugh aloud and was only saved from doing so by the sudden languorous approach of Mrs Perigo, who bore down on him with dark still eyes and swinging hips. Pop knew all about Mrs Perigo, who was wearing a tight evening dress of geranium-leaf green that fitted her like a pod, and he was already on his guard.

'You sort of live next door, don't you?' she said.

Sort of, Pop said. Half a mile along the road.

'Never see you around anywhere. How can that be?'

That, Pop said, could only be because she didn't keep her eyes open, a remark that caused her to give him another slow inviting glance, openly ripe and full.

'I will in future though,' she said.

Pop laughed and then was silent. He wasn't going to be drawn by Mrs Perigo. There were men in every village for a radius of ten miles round who wished with all their hearts they'd never met Corinne Perigo.

'Silly to be so near and never have a peep of anybody,' she said. 'That's the worst of the country though, there's so damn little fun.'

Pop, drinking sherry in sips so minute that he could hardly taste it at all, thought that if any woman had had any fun it was Corinne Perigo, who had in her time run off with a naval commander, a veterinary surgeon, and an agricultural inspector. The naval commander had shot himself and the inspector was in a home. Pop didn't know about the vet, but in the process of her adventures the forbearing Perigo had turned into a monosyllabic horse.

'Heard you say there was no fun in the country.' It was Pinkie Jerebohm, offering a plate of the snippiest of cocktail snippets to Pop and Mrs Perigo. 'Have one of these. And what about your glass?'

What about it? Pop thought and was dismayed to hear Pinkie say as she peered into his glass:

'Oh! you're still all right, I see.'

Pop simply hadn't the heart to say anything and he could only suppose there was so little recognizable difference between a full and an empty thimble that you really couldn't blame her.

'Well,' Mrs Perigo said, 'do *you* think there's any fun?'

'My husband does,' Pinkie lisped. 'He adores it. He thinks the days are so long. Much longer than they are in town, miles longer. Perhaps it's because he's always up with the lark. The only thing is that you can't get help for love nor money. I had to get this Austrian girl in. She can't cook though and even she's been spending her days off in the strawberry fields.'

All would be well, Pop assured her, now that the strawberries, potatoes, and sugar beet were finished. She'd get plenty of help now.

'I profoundly hope so.'

A moment later, over in the fireplace, a heavy gust of wind came down the chimney and erupted in a pungent cloud of birch-smoke, so that Captain Perigo, in the act of trying to get a little warmth into his haunches, seemed visibly to rise up, exposed as on a funeral pyre.

This seemed like a signal for Mrs Jerebohm to muster her chilly guests together, which she did with the simpering of a hen gathering stray chicks.

'Shall we go in? I think we might, don't you? I think all's ready. Shall we? Shall we go in?'

Pop gave his thimble sherry a final despondent glance and then switched his gaze to Ma, who was shivering. Better knock it back, he thought, profoundly glad at the same time that he'd insured himself with three Red Bulls. He didn't care for sherry much at the best of times and he was quite right: it was perfickly obvious there wasn't going to be another.

The dining-room was vast too, with polished oak floors that echoed hollow with every step and a big stone fireplace that sheltered yet another pile of smoking birch. If the air didn't quite take your breath away, Ma thought, it wasn't very much better. It was like a stable in winter-time.

The dining-table looked nice though, she thought. Tall red candles rose from green china bowls filled with scarlet hips and haws. There were rose-pink dinner mats, cut wine glasses, pretty silver salt cellars and butter knives with painted handles, all looking discreet and pleasant under golden candlelight.

Everything looked very *très snob*, Pop thought and only hoped the food would be up to the same standard. He was pretty well starving.

Half a minute later, sitting next to Mrs Perigo, he found himself staring down at a small green glass dish in which reposed a concoction consisting of five prawns, a spoonful of soapy pink sauce, and a sixth prawn hanging over the edge of the glass as if searching for any of its mates that might have fallen overboard. You could have eaten the lot, Pop thought, with two digs of an egg-spoon.

'I hope everybody likes prawn cocktail?' Mrs Jerebohm said. A wind whined and whooped like an owl in the chimney as if giving answer. 'I hope you'll forgive me if I don't join you. I'm not allowed it. I have my yoghurt.'

'Give you gee-up?' Ma said. 'Onions serve me that way too.'

Mrs Jerebohm looked frigid. 'Not exactly. It's my diet. I have to watch it all the time.'

'Ma went on a diet once,' Pop said. 'By the time she'd got the diet down her every morning she was ready for a good square breakfast.'

'Really?' Captain Perigo said. 'I mean to say –'

What Captain Perigo meant to say nobody discovered. Mrs Jerebohm toyed with yoghurt. Pop toyed with a prawn, thinking it tasted more like a bit of last week's cod than anything else he could name. Ma sniffed the chilly air, hoping she might catch a smell of steak or something cooking. She rather fancied steak tonight but she merely felt a sense of denial when she remembered how far away the kitchens were.

Presently Mrs Jerebohm swallowed a pill, washing it down with a glass of cold water, and Mr Jerebohm walked round the table, filling glasses with chilled white wine.

Pop, who had made the prawn cocktail last as long as possible, decided he couldn't put off the end any longer and sucked at the last meagre spoonful just as Mrs Perigo dropped her serviette on the floor.

'Do you mind, Mr Larkin? I've dropped my serviette.'

Pop poked about under the table. The serviette had dropped between Mrs Perigo's not unshapely legs, which were held generously apart. The temptation to caress one of them or even both was a strong one which Pop successfully resisted just in time.

When he finally retrieved the serviette and put it back in her lap he was not surprised to notice that she was eyeing him with a keen but voluptuous sort of disappointment. He wasn't at all sure there didn't seem to be a hint of annoyance there too and with a nippy gesture towards Mr Jerebohm he changed the subject.

'Had many pheasants yet, Mr Jerebohm?'

Mr Jerebohm confessed, with a certain air of annoyance too, that he had, in fact, not had many pheasants. Hardly a damned one.

'Oh?' Pop expressed a most fervent and sympathetic surprise. 'How's that? Thought you had plenty.'

So, confessed Mr Jerebohm, did he. But where did the bounders get to? You could walk all the way to the lake and never see a brace.

'Knocking the stoats off?' Pop said, airily.

What on earth had stoats got to do with it? Mr Jerebohm said.

'And what about jackdaws?' Pop said. 'Eh?' Bigger menace than stoats. 'And magpies?' Bigger menace than jackdaws. 'And hawks?' Bigger menace than the lot. Deadly.

Mr Jerebohm, who didn't know a lark from a sparrow, let alone a magpie from a hawk, sat almost as open-mouthed as Captain Perigo while listening to Pop's fluent recital of the pheasant's countless deadly enemies.

'You mean –?'

'Perfickly obvious,' Pop said. 'Your birds are being taken by summink or other.'

Pop stared hard at Ma as he spoke, but Ma didn't move an eyelash in reply.

'Really?' Captain Perigo said. 'I mean say –'

'No doubt about it,' Pop said. 'You'll have to get among the stoats and things. Won't he, Ma?'

Ma cordially agreed. And the foxes.

'Dammit,' Mr Jerebohm said, 'I thought the hunt took care of the foxes.'

'Half and half,' Pop said. 'The hunt takes care of the foxes and the foxes take care of the hunt.'

'Had a fox fetch a goose the other night,' Ma said. 'Right under our noses.'

'I think we fed 'em too well in the first place,' Mr Jerebohm said. 'They simply didn't want to fly.'

'Never. Got to feed 'em. Got to fatten 'em up a bit,' Pop said. 'After all, what's a pheasant if it's all skin and bone?'

Mr Jerebohm said he simply didn't know; he hadn't even seen one. He hadn't seen a snipe, a deer, a hare, or a damn rabbit either. Had Larkin?

'Caught sight of a few in the distance once or twice,' Pop said. 'Too far off, mostly.'

'Really?' Captain Perigo said.

While all this was going on the blonde Austrian maid had been clearing away the cocktail dishes. She was rather a fresh, pretty little thing, Pop thought, and recalled that he hadn't seen her about the village at all. He must look out a bit more and as she picked up his dish he turned and gave her a short warm smile.

She gave him the hint of a smile in reply and a second later he felt the air between himself and Mrs Perigo positively dry up, parched by a withering glare.

While the girl was out of the room Mrs Jerebohm

daintily swallowed another pill and drank another glass of water. Pop tried the white wine, all flavour of which appeared to have been chilled out in some deep and distant tomb.

'What about wild duck then?' Pop said.

As if unprepared to discuss the subject of wild duck Mr Jerebohm went over to the sideboard and started sharpening the carving knife. No, he said rather tersely, he hadn't seen any wild duck either. He doubted in fact if there were any wild duck about the place. If there were they were damn widely scattered.

'They come and go,' Pop said. 'We had a brace last week, didn't we, Ma? Not much on a wild duck, but they're beautiful with orange sauce. Perfick.'

Tortured by the renewed description of Ma's wild duck with orange sauce, Mr Jerebohm found himself faced with the task of dismembering three small larded partridges brought in on a dish by the Austrian maid. They not only looked on the small side but they seemed, he thought, rather crisp. He gave the girl a look of slightly curt reproval and then with sinking heart proceeded to thrust the carving knife hard into the breast of the first partridge.

Under this first prod the bird gave a sharp leap about the dish. A second made it dance sideways, skating in gravy. The knife grated against bone as hard as ebony, setting Ma's teeth on edge, and with depressing insistence Mr Jerebohm attacked it again. This time it skated into the two other birds, one of which leapt completely from the dish and slithered full circle round the sideboard.

After the Austrian maid retrieved it deftly Mrs Jerebohm called, lisping:

'Not for me, dear, you know I mustn't. I have my peanut *pâté*.'

On Mrs Jerebohm's plate there reposed the smallest portion of brown-grey *pâté*, looking not at all unlike a mouse nibbling at a solitary lettuce leaf. A still smaller portion of grated celery, together with one sliced tomato, covered some part of the rest of the plate and for a few moments Mrs Jerebohm stared at it all either as if in disbelief or as if wondering whether something, possibly, could be missing.

Watching her, Ma thought she had the clue.

'Salt?' she said. 'Looking for the salt?'

'Oh! never salt,' Mrs Jerebohm lisped. 'Salt is absolutely fatal.'

Never? Ma said. She hadn't heard.

'*And* pepper. They both put on more weight than bread. Oh! I never, never eat salt. Never, never pepper.'

'Really?' Captain Perigo said. 'I mean say –'

By this time the first of the partridges, tortuously dismembered by Mr Jerebohm, were coming to table, garnished with frozen peas and game potatoes. The birds looked, if possible, more charred than ever and as each meagre portion was set down in the pool of glass and silver and candlelight Ma's customary epitaph 'Shan't get very fat on this' flashed sadly through her mind. No doubt about it: they wouldn't either.

'Absolutely delicious,' Captain Perigo said, uttering his first real original sentence of the evening.

In return Mrs Perigo gave him a look of flat-iron contempt, as if he were not supposed to utter sentences of originality. His jaw, falling open suddenly, expressed a pained acquiescence that showed no sign of receding until he presently found time to pick up slowly, one by one, three or four peas on the end of a fork. Even these remained for some time poised before the empty gap, in air.

'Anyone going hunting on Thursday?' Mr Jerebohm said.

He hadn't hunted much yet. The mid-week meets were awkward and not, it seemed, very well patronized. These days, it appeared, you couldn't get the chaps.

'I'll be there,' Captain Perigo said. The peas had only just gone in when his mouth opened again.

This time there was no answering look of contempt from Corinne Perigo, who merely half-glanced at Pop and said:

'I know I can't. I've got a perm.'

'You going, Larkin?' Mr Jerebohm said.

Pop, rather uncheerfully, said yes, he thought he might. He was struggling with elastic bits of partridge, longing for a cheese-pudding or something, a steak-and-kidney pie or something, to fill him up. Had to take a day off now and then, he said, and he hadn't hunted once this year.

At this point some instinct made him turn and look at Corinne Perigo, who to his considerable surprise was attacking a piece of rubbery breast of patridge with silent fury. The normally soft, sensuous lips were being bitten hard and white and for the life of him he couldn't imagine why.

One thing he hadn't any doubts about, however, was the partridge. He hadn't the heart to ask if the birds had been shot on the estate. Once, as he struggled to get a mouthful of flesh here and there, he saw Mrs Jerebohm smile at him across the table. Half in sympathy rather than anything else he gave her a warm and winning smile in reply.

78

'Like being in the country?' he said.

'Oh! yes.'

Secretly, in fact, she had begun to hate it. The grounds were still full of thistles and willow-herb. The kitchen garden looked sordid and try as you could you couldn't get help. The locals were independent, rude, and treacherous and it would be late spring before she could have asparagus. Even the Austrian girl, simple and nice as she had been on arrival, had started on the path of rural corruption, thanks largely to the strawberry fields.

'Perfick here,' Pop said. 'Wouldn't change it for no-where else in the world.'

'Never, never want to live anywhere else?' Corinne Perigo said.

'Never,' Pop said and with such resolute finality that Mrs Perigo's lips finally untightened and broke into a smile.

All through the sweet-course, which consisted of ice-cream crowned with a solitary half of walnut, the westerly gale rose in the chimney. Smoke puthered into the fire-place in thicker and thicker clouds, until at last a light grey fog hung about the room. Ma found herself shivering more and more often and began to wonder how soon she could get home and cook herself some good hot eggs and bacon. She wasn't sure she wouldn't jump into a bath too.

'Shall we find more comfortable chairs?' Mrs Jerebohm said, 'and some coffee?'

Through increasing fog, with hollow footsteps, Mrs Jerebohm and her guests filed back to the drawing-room, where Mr Jerebohm began to dispense minute thimbles of crème-de-menthe and brandy.

The Austrian maid was also there, serving coffee and

actually smiling with unexpected pertness at Pop as she said, with her strong accent:

'Sugar? One lump or two?'

'Four,' Pop said and while she was still laughing, went on: 'Are you froggy? From France I mean?'

'I am from Austria.'

'Very nice,' Pop said and was not unastonished, in view of the luscious smile he gave her, to see that she served the four sugar-lumps to him herself, smiling with a separate movement of her lips at each one.

These gestures were not lost on Corinne Perigo, who presently cornered him at a safe distance from the smoking fireplace and said:

'Sorry I won't see you at the hunt, Thursday.'

Pop said he wasn't all that sure he could go. Might not find the time.

'No? I'd go if I could change my perm.'

Pop didn't answer. The hunt really didn't interest him this season. He was very busy and the present crowd were pretty rag-tag-and-bobtail. The country, too thickly wooded, with too many orchards, wasn't really good for hunting either.

Nor did Mrs Perigo interest him very much. Nobody could say he wasn't interested in women; he was ready and willing for them any time you cared to name. But Mrs Perigo wasn't quite his kind. Something about her, more especially the voluptuous glances, irked him. He didn't want to go hunting with her either, one way or the other.

'Well, anyway, even if I can't go,' she said, 'you could drop in for a stirrup-cup in the morning, before you went, couldn't you?'

'Never drink in the mornings.'

'No? Simply can't believe it.'

Captain Perigo drank like nobody's business, starting an hour after breakfast.

'Honest fact,' Pop said, straight-faced as an owl. 'Blood pressure.'

Mrs Perigo gave him another deep, slow smile, this time both disturbing and enigmatic too.

'I suffer from it myself,' she said. 'Sometimes. Depending on circumstances.'

Whatever the circumstances were Pop didn't bother to ask and he was glad to hear Ma's warm, friendly voice inquiring of Mrs Jerebohm:

'Get to know many people since you've been here? Made many friends?'

Mrs Jerebohm was too reticent to point out that her poverty in country friendships was only too well reflected in the number of guests at her dinner table. She had conceived, once, the idea of having eight or ten guests that evening for dinner, or perhaps even a cocktail party, but somehow country people seemed to close themselves up, oyster-like, slow to accept you.

'Not too many,' she confessed. 'I did invite a Miss Pilchester to tea last week, but she didn't even answer my note –'

'Batty,' Mrs Perigo said. 'She probably didn't even open it. Or she wove it into a scarf on her loom.'

Ma, who wouldn't have such remarks at any price, rose to Edith Pilchester's defence swiftly and sharply.

'She's not been well, poor thing. Appendix or something. One of those grumbling ones. The sort you have to put up with because they're not bad enough to have out. I keep telling Pop he'll have to go and massage it for her.'

Ma found her rich loud laugh enveloped in a chilly cloud, out of which Corinne Perigo's voice inquired with slow sarcasm:

'Oh? Does he make a habit of massaging appendices?'

'Oh! he'll massage anything for a lark,' Ma said, laughing in bountiful fashion again. 'He's got a waiting list a mile long.'

The frigidity with which the Jerebohms received this announcement sprang less from shock than confusion, which was not improved by Pop saying, with a fresh laugh, that he'd never massaged an appendix in his life.

'Oh! really?' Captain Perigo said. 'Well, I'm damned.'

'You'll have to come over and have a bite and wet with us one day,' Ma said, 'and meet a few people. We'll get the Brigadier and a few more in one Sunday –'

'That's it,' Pop said. 'We'll knock off three or four geese and Ma'll stuff 'em with sage and onions.'

Painfully in a low voice, Mr Jerebohm said:

'Thank you. We'd be glad to.'

This uncordial acceptance threw another chilling mist over the conversation, which stopped completely for half a minute, until Mrs Jerebohm said:

'I hear you have several children, Mrs Larkin. Your house must be full already.'

'Seven so far,' Ma said. 'Quite a little brood.'

'Little? You mean you'd like to have more?'

'Oh! Pop would,' Ma said. 'There's no holding him back.'

In the cool, smoky drawing-room there was no sound but that of coffee spoons stirring at sugary dregs in cups and a few sharp sniffs from Captain Perigo struggling with some obstruction in his nose.

Almost at once Pop's own nose started to sniff out the increasing chill in the air and he was suddenly half afraid that somebody would soon be asking him and Ma if they were married or not and he turned the conversation smartly.

'Seen any hares at all, Mr Jerebohm?'

Mr Jerebohm confessed stiffly that he hadn't seen any hares. He was about to remark that he thought hares in fact were extinct, like wild duck, deer, pheasant, woodcock, and a lot of other things, but Pop broke cheerfully in with:

'Tell 'em how you do hares, Ma. That French recipe, I mean. The one with burgundy and prunes.' In his sudden enthusiasm for the French way with hares he lifted a hand in air, as if about to strike Mr Jerebohm in warm comradeship in the middle of the back. 'That's a beauty. That'll make your gills laugh.'

The prospect of Mr Jerebohm's gills ever laughing again seemed an utterly remote one. The coffee spoons tinkled emptily again in their cups. Captain Perigo sniffed again and then actually brought out his handkerchief and blew at his nasal obstruction, loudly, with a single trumpet snarl that earned him a fresh look of contempt from Mrs Perigo.

'Play crib?' Pop said with great cheerfulness. 'What about a couple of hands at crib?'

Crib? What was crib? Mr Jerebohm was unfamiliar with crib.

'Card game,' Pop explained. 'Very old card game.'

'Perhaps it's getting a little late for cards,' Mrs Jerebohm started to say and was suddenly saved the necessity of continuing by a violent crash of timber or masonry, or both, somewhere in the region of the back door.

'Getting damn windy,' Captain Perigo said and added that he wasn't sure he liked it.

A moment later the agitated Austrian maid burst into the room to say excitedly that half a tree had fallen on the stable roof and that she was getting very frightened. She wasn't used to such winds. They sounded like the sea.

'Better be going,' Ma said. The sudden opening of the door, bringing a driving draught, had set her shivering again. 'Don't want to get myself steam-rollered under a beech tree. That'd be a jammy mess.'

'Well, be seeing you!' Pop said, as they shook hands all round. 'Thank you, Mrs Jerebohm. Thank you, Mr Jerebohm. Don't get doing anything I wouldn't do.'

Mr Jerebohm received this cheerful advice in further silence. The sound of yet another crashing tree branch startled Pinkie Jerebohm into almost running across the wide baronial hallway with Ma's mink stole and Corinne Perigo's big white sheep-skin jacket, which she clutched closely about her shoulders as she turned to Pop to say:

'Well, don't forget that stirrup-cup. If you can find the time.'

'That's right,' Captain Perigo said. 'Roll up for a noggin at any time.'

After Ma and Pop had driven home under a sky of lashing rain and a falling barrage of autumn boughs, Pop was dismayed to find that television had already closed down

84

and that only Charley and Mariette were still up, studying plans for a bungalow on the kitchen table.

While Ma sipped at a good gin-and-mixed and started to fry eggs and bacon, 'because if I don't eat soon my stomach'll drop out,' Mariette said:

'Ma, we can't quite decide. What do you say? Shall we have one bathroom or two?'

'Oh! two, dear,' Ma said with not the slightest hesitation. 'After all, you might not always want to bath together.' She and Pop quite often did.

For crying out gently, Pop thought What next? He gave Ma a severe and disapproving look which she, over the frying pan, completely ignored. He didn't go much on that lark. It was almost as bad as having separate bedrooms. He stood a fat chance of becoming a grandfather if Ma was going to start putting obstacles like that in Charley's way.

Over the eggs and bacon, together with a few glasses of port, Ma warmed up, saying several times:

'Thought I'd never get the circulation back in my feet. I think I'm going to have a hot bath even now.'

Pop said good idea. He thought he might hop in with her.

'Well, do,' Ma said cordially. 'Why not?'

Ma always got into the bath first, for the simple reason that she displaced such an enormous amount of water that Pop could gauge the depth better when he followed her. Tonight the water-line came almost up to the top of the bath, so that not much more than Ma's handsome dark head, wide olive shoulders and upper bosom was revealed.

'Well, that was an evening,' Ma said. 'I thought I'd never get warm again.'

'Me too.'

Pop was feeling human now. A bath with Ma was about the cosiest, pleasantest thing in the world.

'I shouldn't have thought you were cold,' Ma said, 'with the steamy way that Mrs Perigo kept looking at you. I hope you didn't get any ideas about her?'

'Not my type,' Pop said. 'She's sour.'

Ma, washing her neck and shoulders with a flannel impregnated with special French soap, said she was very glad to hear it and at the same time asked Pop if he could reach the Schiaparelli bath-oil from where it stood on the stool. She'd like a drop more in.

'I'll have to get a bigger size next time,' she said as she peppered the water with a generous spray of oil, 'I use so much of it.'

'Soap at your end?' Pop said.

'Somewhere. Had it a moment ago.'

With adroit hands Pop started a swift search for the soap, but Ma's body occupied such a large space of water that there was very little area left to search in. His hands kept finding Ma instead, so that presently she was half shrieking:

'Sid! If you do that again you'll have me under. You know what happened last time.'

Once Ma had laughed so much that she slid suddenly under, unable to sit up again until Pop climbed out of the bath and pulled her up.

'Sid! I told you. You'll have me under.'

'Got to find the soap, Ma,' Pop said. Ma, all pink and

olive, seemed to him to blossom through hot clouds of perfumed steam. 'Can't very well get clean without the soap.'

'Well, it's not down *there*!'

'No?' Pop said and confessed he was surprised. 'Thought you might be hiding it.'

'What's that against my left foot?' Ma said. 'Is that it? or is it you?'

Slightly disappointed, Pop found the soap beside Ma's left foot, the sole of which he tickled lightly, making her shriek again, so that she slapped him playfully in protest. In return he started splashing her with water, saying at the same time:

'Wonder if Mr and Mrs Jerebohm ever bath together? What do you think, Ma? Doubtful?'

'Never,' Ma said. 'She locks herself in and does exercises. She told me.'

Laughing, Pop said some people never had any fun and started tickling Ma again about the soles of her feet, so that she suddenly wallowed backwards like a huge handsome olive seal, laughing too.

Almost prostrate, she lay for some moments helpless and shrieking, half the global map of her body revealed, until finally with an ecstatic rush of joy, telling himself that this was perfick, Pop stretched out his arms towards the familiar continent of pink hills and olive valleys and fished her up again.

6

By ten o'clock on Thursday morning Pop decided that he wouldn't go to the hunt meeting after all. Something big was brewing up in the way of another Army surplus deal and it would take him most of the day to sift the prospects out. Probably show something like five hundred per cent if it came off: anyway, wurf while.

Nevertheless as he drove away from the house in the Rolls he told himself there could be no harm in stopping off at The Hare and Hounds and saying hello to one or two people, just to see what sort of rabble had turned up. The weather had turned very mild again. The first elm leaves were colouring a clear bright yellow and above them the sky was a sharp northern blue, washed clean of any trace of cloud. If anything it was too blue, Pop thought, and as he got out of the Rolls his hypersensitive nostrils instinctively sniffed the morning air for the smell of rain.

Outside the pub hounds were prancing and snuffling about the paddock, tails raised like a collection of pump handles. A few pink coats loped to and fro. Captain Perigo, blue of chin and already slightly watery eyed, was having a whisky outside the bar door, his hard hat sitting well down on his ruby ears. Mr Jerebohm had turned up too and was clearly not used to riding very much. His pose of squatting on his horse, posterior pushed out like a rudder, looked part of a game of leap-frog.

Corinne Perigo had, after all, also turned out and was talking to a man named Bertie Fanshawe, the man whom

Ma had mistakenly suspected she had run away with. Perhaps Ma had mixed her up with Freda O'Connor, who also often had a fling. She was a girl of spanking bosom and voice of low husky passion who was now talking to Colonel Arbor, a shortish man who rarely talked much but, like a bronchial horse, merely guffawed in a rusty sort of way. Bertie Fanshawe was beefy. You could have cut his face up into prime red steaks. He guffawed too, but brassily, on coarse trumpet voluntaries all his own.

They were a pretty ripe old lot, Pop thought. The cream of county society, eh? It was a good job, he thought, that Mariette had turned out, neat and beautiful as usual, with Montgomery as escort. He was proud of them both. He was glad too to see the Brigadier, though on foot, the poor devil not being able to afford a second-hand motor car, let alone a nag. It would have been pleasant to see Angela Snow appear too but it was, he feared, too much to expect. She lived too far away.

Then, to his great surprise, he saw, less than a minute later, a jeep-drawn horse-box draw up; and out of the jeep, bright as a quince among a collection of sacked potatoes, Angela Snow.

She was a band-box of a girl if you liked, he thought. She even had the knack of being able to choose a horse that perfickly matched herself. Today she was riding a brilliant burning chestnut, lean and silky of body as she was.

It showed Mr Jerebohm's lean black mare up, Pop thought, as rather a poor old bag of bones: an animal with a decidedly uncharitable look in its eye.

'My sweet.' In a moment or two Angela, unabashed by

public gaze, was kissing Pop full on the mouth, to the extreme consternation of the Brigadier, who had not been quite the same man since the passionate upheavals on the hearth-rug, and the unpleasant surprise of Corinne Perigo, who started flashing glances of jagged glass on all sides, blackly. 'Not going to come with us today? Abysmally disappointed.'

Pop, who hadn't seen Angela since the gay evening with the Brigadier, blandly explained that he was only a working man.

'Can't afford the time to go gallivanting. Got to scratch a living somehow. Been up since five as it is.'

'Suppose so. And how's the swimming pool? Coming on?'

Slow, Pop said, slow. They didn't work all that hard these days. The heating apparatus had been held up too.

'You stand there, you croaker, and tell me it's going to be *heated*?'

'Course,' Pop said and laughed in his most friendly, rousing fashion. 'Can't have Ma catching cold.'

'Naturally not. Didn't you murmur something too about having a party to celebrate the opening?'

'In the spring,' Pop said airily. 'In the spring.'

Presently a horn flashed copper in the morning sun, a signal to remind Pop that the hunt would soon be away and that therefore there was precious little time left in which to get outside a snifter.

'Come and have one,' he said. 'We'll get the Brigadier in too.'

He took Angela softly by the arm, steering her through a thickening crowd of people, cars, bicycles, horses, and horse-boxes to the door of The Hare and Hounds, at the same time tapping the Brigadier on the shoulder as he passed him.

'Going to buy you a drink, General old boy,' he said. 'Come on. Angela's here,' and was surprised for the briefest moment not to hear the Brigadier's customary grunt of polite refusal in reply.

Nor had the Brigadier the slightest intention of giving it. A storm of volcanic emotions had swept over him at the mere sight of Angela Snow's lips pressing themselves on Pop's. He knew only too well what that felt like. He could once again feel his hand gyrating on Angela's pulsating naked back. He was overwhelmed by a returning rush of every detail of that stormy session on the hearth-rug. If ever he needed a drink, he thought, it was now.

'First you're coming. Then you're not coming. Fickle man.'

A languorous hand held Pop in check three or four yards from the lounge bar door. It was Corinne Perigo, looking at him in a pretence of friendly calm not confirmed by the fact her nostrils were dilating with unusual quickness.

'Couldn't manage it,' Pop said. 'Business to do.'

'And here am I changing my hair appointment.'

For the life of him Pop couldn't think what that had to do with him and was almost ready to say so when she went on:

'And who's the tall blonde piece? Haven't seen her before.'

'Old flame.'

Pop didn't laugh as he said this, but Mrs Perigo did.

'Old I suppose is right. Still, I see she appeals to the Brigadier too. The poor old thing was having palpitations.'

Pop, suddenly tired of a conversation in which his nearest and dearest friends were being put through a mincer, turned abruptly and went into the bar, leaving a stunned Corinne Perigo standing in lethal silence, alone.

Inside the pub he decided he had a call to pay before joining Angela and the General at the bar. It took him only a couple of minutes to pay it, but meanwhile the Brigadier was glad of even that short respite. It gave him a chance to recall the shattering experience on the hearth-rug.

'Rather an evening we had.'

'Momentous.'

Ever since that time an important gap in his memory had bothered the Brigadier very greatly and with a sudden rush of courage he decided that this was as good a moment as any to fill it in.

'I found myself on the bed,' he said, 'and you not there.'

'A girl has to go home sometime.'

The Brigadier said he knew. But it was the time before she went home he was now referring to.

'You were asleep, darling. Very asleep.'

'And you?'

'I was having that brandy you promised me. I needed it too.'

My God, the Brigadier said, half on fire, had the whole affair had that sort of effect on her?

'Devastating, dear boy.'

The Brigadier, completely on fire now, pitched his voice in a low whispered key, expressing everything in a single cryptic but palpitating sentence.

'Folly to repeat it?'

'What do you think?' Angela said and gave him a long, languid smile.

The Brigadier was saved the necessity of answering this enigmatical question by the breezy entrance of Pop, who floated up to the bar, called the barmaid his little Jenny Wren, ordered himself a double Johnnie Walker and urged Angela and the Brigadier to knock theirs back and quick. The hunt would soon be moving away.

'Wish you were coming,' Angela said. 'Both of you.'

'I'm afraid,' the Brigadier said, 'my hunting days are over.'

'Oh?' she said and laughed on high, belling notes. 'Must have been rather something when you were in full cry.'

The Brigadier felt suddenly half way to heaven again. A late peacock butterfly, roused by the warmth of autumn sun, fluttered at the bar window, danced among the bottles and flew across the room. The Brigadier watched it settle and cling delicately, wing-eyes brilliant, to the edges of a curtain. Nobody could have felt more like a peacock than himself at that moment and it was in a dream that he heard the barmaid say:

'Sounds as if they're moving off, sir. Yes, they are.'

'One for the road,' Pop said and pulled a roll of fivers from his pocket about the size of a pint mug. 'Double for the General. Large Madeira for Miss Snow. Another double for me.'

Already horses were moving off outside. Cars were starting up. A couple of pink coats flashed by. The peacock flew again and Pop said:

'Madeira. Don't think I ever tasted it. Any good?'

'Sweet. And warm without being sordid.'

The Brigadier laughed, alternately watching the butterfly and the edges of Angela Snow's extremely fine smooth hair. The two of them were so beautiful that it positively hurt him to look at them and as he sipped his whisky he wished to God his hunting days weren't over. But, dammit, it was no use, they were; he was past pretending; and he knew the best he would get for the rest of the day would be the far cry of hounds and that queer tugging bleat of a horn being blown across bright autumn fields.

'Well, cheers,' Pop said. 'Down the hatch. Have a wonderful day. Even if you don't kill nothing, I mean.'

It was soon after three o'clock in the afternoon that Mr Jerebohm, with growing discomfort, decided that he was far from having a wonderful day. He thought it was developing, on the contrary, into a hellishly unpleasant day. Unlike the Brigadier, he was beginning to wish his hunting days were over. As rain began to fall, at first in mere biting spits, then in a steady chilling downpour, he even started to wish they had never begun.

It wasn't merely that the countryside, under teeming rain, looked and felt more uncharitable with every step he took. The hunt wasn't running very true to form either.

He knew perfectly well what a hunt ought to look like. He had seen it so often in old prints, on Christmas cards and in advertisements for whisky. It was gay; it positively bounced with cheerful life. Against charming rural backgrounds of woodland and pasture, in winter weather always crisp and beautiful, riders and hounds galloped at full invigorated stretch, all together, well-drilled as an army, in pursuit of a small red animal framed against the far blue sky. The pink coats were as bright as holly-berries at Christmas-time and the laughing tails of the hounds as happy as children at play.

But today there was nothing cheerful or well-drilled or invigorating about it. Not only was the rain becoming colder, drearier, and heavier every moment; there was something very wrong with his horse. He had bought it under the impression that it was a hunter; he had paid what he thought was a stiffish price for it; he liked its colour.

Pinkie liked its colour too; she even thought it handsome. There had even been a time, a day or two since, when Mr Jerebohm had thought it handsome too, but now he could have cheerfully hit it with a shovel.

All day the animal had behaved like an engine without steam; it continually lacked the power to pull itself off dead centre. After desultory canters of thirty or forty yards or so it would suddenly draw up, give a congested cough in its throat and then release breath in hollow bursts of pain. Afterwards it stood for some time staring with cautious eyes at the dripping hedgerows, autumn woods, and bare, sloppy stubbles before, with amazing instinct, turning for home.

It had been, in fact, turning for home all day. Three times during the morning Mr Jerebohm had been blisteringly cursed with words such as 'If you can't keep up bloody well keep out of the way!' From time to time he found himself several hundred yards, even half a mile, behind the pack. He was continually losing hounds behind distant woods, where they wailed like lost souls, mocking him. Several times he got off and walked. It seemed quicker that way.

By half past three in the afternoon he knew, with miserable certainty, that he was lost. Pack and riders were nowhere to be seen. It was raining more and more fiercely on a driving wind and his horse held its blowing frame like a sieve to the rain. Mr Jerebohm, in fact, felt like a sieve himself. The rain was driving large holes through his face, chest, legs, shoulders, and buttocks, and the wind, colder every moment, followed the rain.

A growing conviction that the countryside was one big, evilly devised swindle started to come over him as he turned his horse to the west, the direction where he thought home lay. The supposed pastoral nature of it was a ghastly myth. The deer, pheasant, wild duck, hares, and snipe were all a myth too. The fox itself was a myth. There was no such animal. It was extinct, like the dodo. People rode to hounds merely in the hope of seeing the resurrected ghost of one.

Soaked to his chest, he crossed an unfamiliar piece of country that seemed like a barren land, a heath with neither hedgerows nor fences, roads, nor telegraph wires. Occasionally Pop Larkin cantered over it with Mariette; it was open and quiet and Pop thought it perfick. Groups of pine covered the farthest slopes. Young birches, yellow with late autumn now, had sown themselves among brown acres of bracken. In summer cotton grass blew like snow among pink and purple heather.

Travelling across it on his breathless horse, Mr Jerebohm merely thought it harsh and uncivilized. It was another part of the great country swindle. It was wild, miserable, and shelterless. Oh! for a hot bath, he kept thinking, God, for a hot bath.

On a road at last, under the civilized protection of tele-graph wires, he heard a car coming up behind him in the rain. A second later his horse reared, gave a skyward flip and threw him. He landed heavily on a grass verge that, though soft and sodden with rain, felt as hard as a cliff of rock.

It was Pop Larkin who ran forward, hailed him, got him to his feet and tried to comfort him with the words:

'Lucky you fell on grass, Mr Jerebohm. Might have been a bit hard if you'd gone the other way. Had a good day?'

Dispirited and shaken, Mr Jerebohm merely groaned.

'Better come in to my place and have a drink,' Pop said. 'It's only just down the road. I'll mix you an Old King Cole.'

What the hell, Mr Jerebohm asked himself and then Pop, was an Old King Cole?

'New drink I found the other day,' Pop said. 'Mostly rum. It'll put fire into you.'

Mr Jerebohm groaned again. He didn't want fire put into him. In terrible pain, he was sure his back was split in two. He was convinced his kidneys were ruptured and that his spleen was not where it ought to be. Trying to limp back to his horse he felt one leg give a crack under-neath him and could have sworn that it was broken.

In sympathy Pop said: 'Tell you what. You drive the Rolls back. It's perfickly easy – gears are as smooth as butter. I'll ride the horse.'

Mr Jerebohm, too far gone in agony to argue with this

or any other solution, merely dragged his creaking body into the Rolls and let Pop recapture the horse, which reared again in ugly fashion as he did so.

'See you in five minutes,' Pop said. 'Ma's there.'

He seized the bridle and looked the horse firmly in the face. Not only was it an uncharitable animal to look at, he thought, it was downright ugly. It wanted teaching a sharp lesson. It needed a damn good clout and he promptly gave it one, so that the horse, enormously surprised, at once calmed down.

'Nothing but a bag o' horse meat,' Pop said. 'D'ye hear me?'

At the house he found Mr Jerebohm standing in front of the kitchen fire, a glass of rum in his hand, steaming gently. Ma had also given him a good big wedge of cheese and bacon tart, on which he was now chewing slowly but with silent gratitude. Ma had been deeply sympathetic about the fall. She thought she didn't like the look of him all that much and she was just saying, as Pop came in:

'You look a bit peaky, Mr Jerebohm. It's shaken you up. Why don't you sit down?'

Mr Jerebohm knew he couldn't sit down. He felt that if he did sit down he would never get up again. His bones would lock.

'Shall I telephone the doctor?' Ma said. 'I think I ought.'

In low murmurs Mr Jerebohm said no, he didn't think so; he merely wanted to go home.

'Get outside that one,' Pop said, looking into Mr Jerebohm's glass, 'and I'll mix you another.'

Gratefully Mr Jerebohm got outside the remainder of his Old King Cole. He was steaming more noticeably every moment. His riding boots were half full of water. His ribs ached every time he drew breath and only Pop's large rum cocktail, mixed double as usual to save time, gave him any sort of comfort.

It was the warm rum too that started his brain slowly working again and presently caused him to remember something. It was probably just one more example of the big country swindle, he thought, but he would soon find out.

'Most grateful to you, Larkin,' he said. 'By the way, I've got a bone to pick with you.'

'Pick away,' Pop said. 'Perfickly all right.'

'Didn't you tell me when I bought Gore Court,' Mr Jerebohm said, 'that there was a boat on the lake?'

'Perfickly true,' Pop said, laughing. 'But it ain't there now.'

'Oh? So you know? Then where is it?'

'In my boathouse,' Pop said. 'Just before you took over the house Montgomery found a gang of kids throwing bricks at it, so we rowed it up the lake, carried it over the sluice-gates and brought it up the river. It's safer under cover. I meant to have told you.'

Mr Jerebohm listened in silence, but nevertheless didn't want to seem ungrateful. The rum was marvellously comforting.

'I'll row it back in the spring,' Pop said. 'I daresay Montgomery'll give it a coat of varnish in the meantime.'

Overwhelmed with kindness, Mr Jerebohm could still find nothing to say. Nor, for another moment or two, had he any words to answer another remark of Pop's, who presently disappeared into the pantry and came out holding a brace of pheasants.

'Little present for you,' he said. 'Knocked 'em off in the medder last Monday afternoon. They'll want hanging a couple o' days.'

Searching for words, Mr Jerebohm felt he could have wept. 'Wonderfully kind,' was all he managed to mutter. 'Very, very kind.'

'Make a nice change from pills and diets,' Ma said, 'won't they? I don't hold with all those pills. The world takes too many pills by half.'

It damn well did too, Mr Jerebohm thought, it damn well did too.

Blessed with pheasants and rum and Pop's final injunction 'to clout the bounder if he plays up again,' he managed to ride slowly home in the dying light of an afternoon across which, at last, the rain was slackening.

There was even a break of light in the west and as he rode past The Hare and Hounds, with the pheasants slung across the saddle, he could distinctly see the faces of Corinne Perigo and Bertie Fanshawe as they cantered slowly past him.

'Good night!' they called and he said 'Good night' in reply, having just enough strength to raise a hand in courtesy to his hat.

'By God,' Bertie Fanshawe said to Mrs Perigo, 'they shoot 'em from horseback now, do they?' The unexpected vision of a man riding home from a fox-hunt with a brace of pheasants slung across his horse was altogether too much to bear. Dammit, it wasn't the thing. 'Next thing you know we'll be having electric hounds and mechanical horses or some damn lark.'

Mr Jerebohm, if he could have heard, might well have thought it a good idea, especially about the horses. As it was he merely limped on towards home, silently aching from boots to collar, wind-stung eyes on the sky.

Unfamiliar though he was with the passage and change of country seasons he knew perfectly well that it was winter that now stared at him out of a cold watery sunset, and that it looked, if possible, even more uncharitable than the rain, his horse, and the darkening countryside.

7

WALKING slowly along the lakeside on a shimmering afternoon in late April, the warmest so far of the year, Pinkie Jerebohm saw in the middle distance across the water a floating object, pale primrose in colour, to which for some moments she was unable to give a name.

After staring at it steadfastly for some time, just as incapable as Mr Jerebohm of detecting the difference between one bird and another, she finally decided that it must be, of all things, a yellow swan. She had always supposed that swans were white, but perhaps they turned yellow in the mating season or something of that sort. You never knew with nature.

A few moments later, to her intense surprise, the yellow swan started waving a hand. A sudden impulse made her wave in reply and it took her only a few seconds longer to realize that whatever changes of colour nature might effect in swans at spring-time it worked no such miracles on Pop Larkin.

Pop, gay in a yellow sports shirt, hatless, and fully ready to greet the first fresh burst of spring, was rowing Mr Jerebohm's promised boat, gay itself with new golden varnish, across the middle of the lake. The day was absolutely perfick for the job, as he had told himself over and over again that morning. It couldn't possibly have been more perfick: cuckoos calling everywhere, the sky quivering with larks, the woods rich with blackbird song, his favourite of all except the nightingale's. Even the wood-doves were talking softly away on those wooing notes that were the first true voice of summer.

'Afternoon, Mrs Jerebohm!' Pop's voice was quick as a leaping fish as it crossed the water. 'Perfick day. Decided I'd bring the Queen Mary back. Sorry to have been so long.'

It was most kind of him, Pinkie lisped as she watched him ship oars and let the boat drift into the bank. But there really hadn't been that much of a hurry. You couldn't say it had been much like boating weather, could you?

'Perfickly true,' Pop said. 'It is today, though. You'll have to get Mr Jerebohm to give you a trip round the lake before dark.'

Mr Jerebohm wasn't at home, Pinkie said. Moreover she wasn't at all sure that he rowed.

'Pity,' Pop said. 'Very nice little boat.' With a neat half-wink he invited Mrs Jerebohm to give the fresh-varnished boat the once-over. Montgomery, he thought, had done a very good job on her. 'Even had the carpet-sweeper on the cushions.' The cushions, a bright plum-purple with lemon pipings, looked very gay and spring-like too.

'Like me to give you a trip?' Pop said. Perky as a terrier, he skipped from boat to bank, where he tied the painter to a tree-root, laughing freely. 'Beautiful afternoon for it – might never get another one like it for weeks.'

Pinkie Jerebohm, who was dressed in a close-fitting lavender jersey suit that only succeeded in showing how fruitless all her fond hard work at slimming had been, said that she had, as a matter of fact, actually started out to look for primroses.

'Come to the right place,' Pop said and with an extensive sweep of a hand enthusiastically indicated the woods that came down to the very edge of the shimmering lake at its farthest end. 'Woods are full of 'em. Crowded. Fick as fick. You can even smell 'em as you go by. Hop in. I'll take you over.'

Mrs Jerebohm hesitated. She wasn't at all sure about hopping in. She had Corinne Perigo coming in to tea at four o'clock and what time was it now?

Impressively Pop's wrist-watch flashed gold in the sun. 'Only three o'clock,' he said. 'Bags o' time.'

For another apprehensive second or two Mrs Jerebohm hesitated. Among other things was the boat safe? It didn't leak or anything of that kind? She couldn't swim. She was, in fact, terrified of water.

'Pity,' Pop said. 'I mean about the swimming. Oh! the boat's perfickly safe.' After a succession of unobtrusively quick glances at Pinkie's figure, he decided that, slimming or no slimming, she wasn't at all bad in the right places and would probably look quite passable in a bathing costume. 'Thought you might like to come over and use our swimming pool when we get it open next month. Lovely pool. All blue tiles.'

Mrs Jerebohm thanked him for thinking of her, but said that it wasn't all that much fun, was it, if you couldn't swim?

'Ma can't swim,' Pop said, 'but she has fun all right. Trust Ma. Come over one afternoon and I'll learn you. In a couple o' days I'll have you going.'

Well, Pinkie said, she didn't know about that. Though she didn't say so there were, after all, limits. There were certain proprieties. Mr Jerebohm wasn't often home in the afternoons and he mightn't think it quite nice if his wife took swimming lessons with Larkin when he wasn't there.

'Good for your figure,' Pop said, with some enthusiasm and several more rapid glances at it. 'Not that it's not good now.'

An unusual flutter sprang through Pinkie Jerebohm. Some seconds later, almost without knowing it, she was accepting Pop's offer of a hand and in a fraction of a minute afterwards she was in the boat, facing Pop, who began rowing her away.

'But you *will* keep an eye on the time, won't you?' she said. 'What I mean is – I mean I must absolutely dove-tail in with Corinne. I simply mustn't keep her waiting.'

Damn Corinne, Pop thought, determined not to spoil a perfick afternoon worrying about Corinne, who several times during the winter had put his back up in no uncertain way. At the Hunt Ball, at two o'clock in the morning, she had cornered him in a half-lit draughty corridor on the pretext of getting him to take out a subscription to a new country club about to be started up by Bertie Fanshawe. In reality it was merely an excuse to start pawing his neck. On an evening in January she had somehow winkled him out of the bar of The Hare and Hounds on the pretext that her car wouldn't start. On that occasion, without ceremony, she began pawing him all over and then turned like a snake, actually hissing, when he told her to stop it and quick. 'You need a good belting,' he told her on a third occasion, when she telephoned twice in one evening to invite him over for a drink because the Captain was away. That, she told Pop with savage sweetness, was exactly what she hoped he was going to give her. She wouldn't rest, in fact, until he did.

She'll rest a devil of a long time, Pop thought and a second later put Corinne Perigo completely from his mind by asking Pinkie Jerebohm if she could smell the primroses yet? In his own hypersensitive way he had already caught the lightest breath of them across the water.

'No,' she said and in fact the boat was already drifting in to the far bank, where young hazel and sweet chestnut and a few high, gold-flowered oaks came down to the water's edge, before she actually detected the first scent of them floating on the lightest of airs.

'Wonderful scent,' Pop said. 'Fancy there's a few blue-bells there too.' He drew deep breaths, with selective sharpness. Yes, you could smell the bluebells too. 'Get 'em?'

Pinkie Jerebohm, helped out of the boat by Pop's two outstretched hands, had to confess that she couldn't get them. It was all too elusive for her. It was wholly impossible to separate one scent from another, especially when she scarcely knew which was which, and suddenly at the woodland's edge she was deeply aware again of an uncommonly nervous flutter darting through her, leaving her slightly uncertain at the knees.

For the rest of the afternoon, at irregular intervals, she kept experiencing that same sensation without ever being able to decide what caused it. Crowds of white anemones and primroses covered the whole floor of the wood with endless drifts of the softest unwinking white and yellow stars. The tops of the trees were gold-green belfries of bud pouring down bird-song in tireless peals. From across the lake cuckoos called continually, bell-like too, the notes taken up, transformed, and repeated in the wooing moan of doves that Pop adored so much.

Pinkie, bending among primroses, sometimes even kneeling among them on patches of big dry papery chestnut leaves, gradually felt intoxicated and absorbed to a point where time no longer mattered. Nor did Pop remind her. It was pretty nearly perfick by the lakeside on such a day. It was his idea of heaven. The only thing that could perhaps have made it more perfick still, he thought, was the chance of having a short, gentle squeeze with Pinkie.

He wondered how she'd take it? Just the same as Edith Pilchester did? he wondered, and then suddenly found he couldn't be sure. They were rather *très snob*, the Jerebohms. She might go sour.

Still, a casual brush among the primroses, accidental or otherwise, would soon tell him. Couldn't do no harm. It wasn't every girl, after all, who got the chance of being stroked in the middle of a primrose wood on a hot April afternoon.

Several times afterwards he found himself watching the bending, rounded figure of Pinkie, plumpish and smoothly tight in its lavender jersey suit in spite of all her slimming, and told himself that the time had surely come when a little bit of dove-tailing might be fun.

Each time she suddenly straightened up and walked away. Each time, too, he told himself he couldn't be absolutely sure about her. Something about the big bunches of primroses that she had gathered and now held in front of her as she walked gave her an odd look of innocence that he couldn't quite get over.

All this time he himself had been gathering violets, mostly fat white ones, but also a score or two of the dark purple kind. Every now and then he buried his nostrils in them, draining them of scent. All the nerves of the spring afternoon seemed to vibrate tautly as he smelled the flowers and once he felt impelled to call out:

'Beautiful, ain't it? Nowhere like the country.'

Pinkie, who was now gathering separate bunches of white anemones, said she agreed, though in fact the winter hadn't taught her so. The winter had been a trial, hard to bear. That was largely because Mr Jerebohm still insisted on living in Gore Court not because it was pleasant, convenient, or in any way desirable but merely as a means of losing money. Mr Jerebohm in fact was now raising pigs. Palatial sties had sprung up everywhere and Mr Jerebohm found a certain satisfaction in feeding the animals on pigswill made of gold. Pinkie, who didn't understand the reasoning behind making money on the Stock Exchange and giving it to pigs to eat in the country, couldn't help feeling she would have preferred a maisonette on the front at Brighton, where she could occasionally parade in her best hat, gossip over morning coffee, and gaze at the sea.

Here there was hardly anyone to gossip with except Corinne Perigo. The natives, she thought, were uncommonly hostile. They kept themselves steadfastly to themselves. Friendliness seemed no part of their nature. The Austrian maid had left two weeks ago in a huff and now, with the arrival of spring, all the women of the village were planting potatoes, hoeing strawberries or doing strange jobs in hop-fields. She knew now that she couldn't get any help for months and suddenly as she thought of it for the fiftieth time that week she gave a long, uncertain sigh.

Pop, hearing it from some distance off, came over to her bending figure, carrying his bunch of white and purple violets like an offering.

'Surely not sighing on an afternoon like this?' he said. 'Too perfick by half for that. Smell the violets.'

Laughing, he thrust the violets up to Pinkie Jerebohm's face and for a delicious second or two she dreamed over them, drinking scent. Broken sunlight fell like a light veil on her face, which was not unpretty in its simpering way, and on her two hands, clasping almost more primroses and anemones than they could safely hold.

This, Pop told himself, might be just the moment for a trial run. Perhaps he should try her under the chin first and see what happened? But suddenly Pinkie, from being almost completely unbalanced one moment in scent and sun and flowers, darted out of herself with a lisping exclamation:

'Oh! you know it's really awfully awfully sweet of you to bring me over here. I do appreciate it. Spending so much of your valuable time –'

Pop, still locked in indecision, uncertain whether to brush her lightly under the chin or go in for a proper squeeze where there'd be no mistaking what it meant, hadn't a second longer in which to make up his mind before she almost threw up her flower-crowded hands in the air.

'Time! But whatever time is it, pray? We must have been here half an hour or more.'

Pop, laughing, flashed a look at his watch and said:

'More like hour and a half. It's nearly half past four.'

'Oh! my goodness. Corinne will be frantic!'

To Pop's intense surprise Pinkie broke into running, actually dropping flowers as she scurried under the trees to the water-side. He followed her on light springy steps, hoping she might possibly slip and fall in a harmless sort of way so that he could have the pleasure of picking her up but to his disappointment she made the boat without a trip or stumble.

A moment later he was there too, catching her lightly by the soft upper flesh of her arm as he helped her into the boat. To his further surprise a couple of extra velvety squeezes had no effect at all on Pinkie, who seemed utterly oblivious not only of Pop but of everything else as she half-stumbled into the boat and flopped rather heavily down on the plum and yellow cushions.

'Don't rock the boat,' Pop said.

'Whatever can I have been thinking about? An hour and a half! Whatever *was* I thinking?'

Pop, taking up the oars and quietly starting to row the boat out into the lake, where silver shoals of small fry were leaping up like little fountains in the sun, noticed that Pinkie in her haste and distraction hadn't had a moment in which to put her dress straight. Her lavender skirt had ridden up well above her knees.

Charmed and slightly excited by the unexpected vision of Pinkie's rather plump silky legs, Pop found himself paying less and less attention to her lisping self-chastisement as he rowed her across the lake in the sun. Except that he damned once or twice the irritating and oppressive entry of Corinne Perigo into the conversation he was enjoying himself very much, both actually and in anticipation.

Pinkie, he decided, wasn't half a bad shape after all. Her legs were quite pretty and he could see an awful lot of them.

'I'll never, never forgive myself. It really is a granny knot, isn't it? Inviting people to tea and then just not being there. Oh! I *am* a careless fool.'

'You'll be at the house in ten minutes,' Pop said, full of airy comfort. 'Women are always late anyway.'

'That remark doesn't help,' Pinkie said. The social strain, keeping her at full stretch, almost made her voice break. 'You don't see any sign of Corinne, I suppose?'

No, Pop said and told himself that he was damned if he wanted to. There was something crude about that woman. After all, as Ma often said, you had to have a bit of finesse about you.

The boat was still thirty yards from the opposite bank when Pinkie, hands full of flowers, sat forward on her cushions with all the appearance of a frog ready to leap.

'You wouldn't mind awfully if I absolutely made a dash for it, would you?'

Not much time now, Pop thought. The golden afternoon was slipping away. His chances were disappearing as rapidly and surely as the boat was drifting through shoals of unfurling water-lily pads into the bank.

'Sit still,' Pop said. 'Don't stand up.' Pinkie had actually, in her anxiety, tried to stand up in the boat. 'Wait till I tie her up. You don't want a wet tail, do you?'

Utterly oblivious of her risen skirt, Pinkie sat on the very edge of the cushion, an inch or so of bare thigh revealed above her stockings.

Now or never, Pop told himself. 'Don't move until I say,' he warned her. 'It's a bit deep just here.'

Momentarily calmed by sensible advice, Pinkie sat precariously still on her cushion while Pop, yellow shirt fluttering, nipped on to the bank and pulled the boat in.

'Hold hard till I tell you!'

A second offering of sensible advice was completely lost on Pinkie, who suddenly leapt up, staggered forward to the bank and into the unready arms of Pop, who still had the boat's rope in his hands. Staggered too, Pop dropped the rope, felt Pinkie begin to slip down the grassy slope towards the lake and managed to catch her firmly with both arms, just in time.

'Neat bit o' rescue work,' Pop thought and in a moment had Pinkie in a swift and uncompromising embrace, at the same time caressing her with one hand some inches below the back waistline.

For some moments a light but intoxicating perfume of half-crushed violets, primroses, and anemones filled the air and Pinkie, almost breathless, gasped as she caught at it. At the same time her lisping mouth half opened in what Pop thought was a gesture of encouragement. Stimulated, he gave the roundest part of one thigh an extra nip of affection and was on the point of kissing her full on the lips when, to his pained surprise, she started screaming madly.

He hadn't ever heard anyone, he thought, scream quite so loud. You could surely hear it a mile away. On high, full-throated notes Pinkie lifted her face to the sky and for nearly half a minute wailed wordlessly, at the same time dropping every flower she held.

'Better try to comfort her a bit I suppose,' Pop thought and was just wondering how to start this delicate operation when he saw a new figure running towards him along the lakeside.

It was Corinne Perigo, advancing in a hatless charge.

'Wherever have you been? Whatever has happened?'

Pinkie Jerebohm, white-faced, standing in a pool of stricken flowers, allowed herself a moment of deathly silence before answering in a whisper:

'This man has just tried to violate me.'

Pop had hardly grasped the words before Corinne Perigo gave him a venomous, curdling look.

'You absolute swine,' she said. 'You absolute swine.'

Pop, for once, was at a loss for an effective reply. No one had ever called him that before. It was rather much, he thought. A moment later he was startled to hear Corinne Perigo's voice again, now speaking in tones of even colder venom.

'Have him charged, Pinkie. Put him in court. Let the police deal with him. The swine. It's high time. I'll be a witness for you.'

As a weeping, flowerless Pinkie was led away along the lakeside Pop found himself staring with mild disconsolation at the lake, dismayed to find that the boat, which he hadn't had time to tie up, was drifting away.

One way or another, it was a bad end to a perfick afternoon.

'Not sure you haven't gone and torn it this time, Sid,' he told himself. 'Not sure you haven't gone and torn it now.'

8

ON that same shimmering April afternoon Edith Pilchester, succumbing at last to the grumbling appendix that had been troubling her for weeks, went into hospital to have it out. When Ma heard of this nearly a week later she was not only full of sympathy for the wool-gathering Edith, always so lonely, but at once urged that Pop must pay her a visit as soon as possible, at the same time taking something nice with him to cheer the poor thing up.

'You'd be worth a dozen boxes o' pills to her. She'd be up and about in no time.'

Pop agreed and presently, on a showery April evening full of thrush song, took Edith Pilchester two bottles of port, a basket of fresh peaches, pears, grapes, and apricots, a box of milk chocolates, a large bunch of deep yellow freesias and several slices of cold breast of turkey. All spring came flowing richly into Edith's room on the strong fragrance of freesias and Edith, pale and meagre, wept.

This, Pop said, they couldn't have; it wouldn't do at all; and immediately sat down on the bed and held her hand. This warm and unexpected gesture merely had the effect of making Edith weep afresh, not quietly now but in a loud, spinsterish blubber, so that soon, when a nurse came in to fuss with a chart, there was cold severity in the air.

'And what,' she said, 'have you been doing to my patient?'

'Making love to her,' Pop said, quick as a jackdaw.
'Like a sample?'

'That will do. I must ask you not –'

'See what he's brought me!' Edith Pilchester sobbed.
'Freesias. Wine. Gold, frankincense, and myrrh –'

The effect of this outburst was so touching that the nurse
suddenly felt like weeping too and hastily remembered she
had something to do in another ward.

When Pop now suggested that Edith should dry her
eyes and have a grape or something she said no, no, no
thank you, she couldn't touch a thing.

'Have a drink then,' Pop said and immediately poured
out half a tumbler of red port, advising Edith to get it
down her at once, so as to warm the vital parts.

Edith, taking the port in one quivering hand and dabbing
her eyes on the corner of her flannelette nightgown with
the other, apologized several times, begging that Pop
wouldn't think her too silly, and said it wasn't merely that
the gifts had overwhelmed her. It was a combination of
things.

'Oh?' Pop said. 'For instance what?'

'I heard the most awful news about you. It was absolutely ghastly.'

Awful news? Pop, cheerful as ever, couldn't think what
that could be.

'This awful woman. This Mrs Jerebohm. They tell me
you're actually being prosecuted.'

Pop laughed with a bucolic sort of bark that actually
reached the young nurse in another ward.

'Oh! that,' Pop said. 'That's a real lark, that is.'

'But *did* you – I mean *is* there any truth in it?'

115

'Course,' Pop said. 'Case comes up in two weeks' time.'

'Ghastly,' Edith said. 'Absolutely ghastly.'

Pop, treating the matter with renewed levity, wondered if Edith would mind all that much if he joined her in a glass of port? With bird-like joy, tears drying now, Edith begged him to do so, adding:

'But what *is* it all about? What *are* you supposed to have done?'

Pop, still sitting on the bed, adroitly poured himself a glass of port.

'Pinched her bottom. She was getting out of a rowing boat.'

Edith, half way between tears and laughter, could only give a frog-like croak in answer, silently wishing it might have been her. No such opportunities had come her way for some time, not even at Christmas.

'But aren't you at all *concerned*? You don't seem to be worried about it one little *bit*.'

Pop, she thought, seemed to be taking life in a spirit of jollier, livelier levity than ever. Incorrigible, remarkable man.

'I'll worry when the time comes,' Pop said. It was a major part of his rather loosely made philosophy to cross bridges when he came to them. 'After all, anything might happen before then.'

It might indeed, Edith thought. It might indeed.

'I only hope,' she said, 'you've got a good solicitor?'

Pop, purporting to be utterly unconcerned, gave her one of his sudden smoothly mischievous glances that had the immediate effect of making her toes tingle sharply at the bottom of the bed.

'Going to conduct the case myself,' he said. He laughed rousingly, winking. 'Counsel for the defence – that's me.'

Edith, sipping port, didn't know whether to be alarmed or delighted.

'But do you know *how*? I *mean* –'

'Seen it all on telly!' Pop assured her blandly. 'Court cases nearly every night of the week on telly.'

'But how you *dare*! I should *die*.'

'Well, I shan't. Going to enjoy myself that day. Drink up.'

Edith drank up, raising her glass to Pop at the same time.

'I can only wish you all possible success,' she said, looking Pop straight in the face with a refreshed swallow-like glance, eyes glowing. 'Oh! I *know* it will be. I *feel* it. I've got that sort of *thing* about it.'

Whole thing would go like a bomb, Pop said. Would she be well enough to be there? He hoped so.

'I shall be there if it *kills* me. And so will all your friends. We'll absolutely *band* together.'

Such fervent promises of support had Pop chuckling again. With charm he started lightly urging Edith to peel herself a grape or a peach or something. In reply Edith had to confess, as she gulped down deep rich breaths of freesia perfume, that she was really altogether too nervous to eat anything for the moment.

Something, she said, biting her lips, had just come to her.

'Oh?' Pop said and looked at her bitten lips with concern, wondering if perhaps she had had a sudden post-operative twinge.

'I've just thought that if it could be of any help at all I'd

117

cheerfully appear as a witness,' she said. 'I mean as to character or something –'

Or something? Pop thought. Good old Edith. Very nice of Edith. But he wasn't sure about that something.

'Haven't quite got the case worked out yet,' he said. 'Haven't got the order of battle ready.'

Edith, who was sure it was going to be absolute battle royal when it came, suddenly felt herself go unreasonably coy. She shrank perceptibly into her nightgown, feeling her toes tingle sharply again at the bottom of the bed.

'By the way, what *are* you charged with? I've asked myself over and over again.'

'Indecent assault or summat,' Pop said. 'It's all in the summons.'

The word indecent immediately seemed to whirr and flash about the room like a dragon-fly on a hot afternoon, making Edith flush in her throat. She knew perfectly well now that all night long she would lie awake and wonder about what could possibly have happened in that rowing boat.

'I never have liked that Mrs Jerebohm,' she said. 'Such people don't belong in the country.'

Oh! old Pinkie wasn't bad, Pop said. You could hardly blame Pinkie. It was Corinne Perigo that was the snake in the grass.

'That woman!' Edith said. 'I could kill her!'

The magisterial vehemence of this remark made her suddenly flop back on the pillows, surprised, flushed, and weakened. Pop had to confess to himself that he was surprised too. It was very strong stuff for Edith. Probably the drink had got into her, like it sometimes did into Charley.

'It's women like her who bring disgrace on our sex,' she said. 'They make you – oh! I don't know *what* they make you –!'

Edith, completely crimson in the face now, broke off helplessly, impotent to express another thought. Pop, slightly alarmed that she might start up a temperature or have a relapse of some sort, urged her to take it easy, at the same time holding her hand.

'Easy,' he urged her softly. 'Easy. Easy.'

Easiness came to Edith Pilchester in the form of a long quiet thrill. The last deep sigh before sleep could never have quietened her more effectively than that single repeated word or the clasping of Pop's hands.

'Got to trot along now,' Pop told her some time later. 'Come and see you again soon.'

Light cold April showers were falling on the window. The cloud that dropped them was slate-dark, bringing on an early twilight in which the freesias, the peaches, and the apricots all glowed a curious, almost phosphorescent orange.

In a low voice, though not tired, Edith several times thanked Pop for coming. He would be very much in her thoughts, she said. Very much. Never, in fact, out of them.

Pop, who had made up his mind to treat her to a good-night kiss, then remembered something himself.

'Forgot to tell you about our swimming pool. Going to have a party when we open it next month. What about a donkey race in the water? Eh? Men and girls?' He laughed with his customary carelessness. 'That's if they don't put me inside.'

'Inside?' Her mind vibrated madly with alarm. 'You don't mean prison?'

He meant prison, Pop said. Well, why not? It was warm. It was free. He believed they even had telly there too nowadays.

'Awful man,' she said. 'I believe you're really trying to frighten me.'

'Not on your nelly,' Pop said and a second later, pressing her back on the pillows, gave her a faultless dream of a kiss that couldn't have acted more like a sedative, so much so that when the nurse came back, twenty minutes later, she found Edith peacefully sleeping, the half-drunk glass of port still in her hands.

'Visitor for you,' Ma said, when Pop reached home half an hour later. 'And I'll bet you'll never guess who.'

Pop could guess all right; he knew.

'Sergeant Buzz-whiskers.'

Sergeant Wilson, that was. He was the policeman who had originally served the summons. Hated doing it to Sid, he confessed, but there it was. Duty.

'Well, it's not the sergeant,' Ma said. 'That's caught you.'

It had caught him too, Pop said, and after two or three guesses decided he might just as well go into the sitting-room and see for himself while mixing a decent pick-me-up at the same time.

He had hardly decided on this before a small figure, not unlike Pop but twenty years older, nipped into the kitchen. He looked very much like an artful grey terrier who had spent a lifetime gnawing an infinite number of bones, a practice that had knocked several of his front teeth out. His bony yellow forehead had a perceptible hollow in the centre of it. If by some chance this had been filled with a third eye it could hardly have increased the strong magnifying qualities of the rest of his face. The lively little grey eyes were telescopic lenses, picking up every detail. The ears were bulbous earphones, tuned to every breath.

'Uncle Perce!' Pop said. 'Haven't seen you since Mariette's wedding day.'

Uncle Perce, in a voice no less diamond-sharp than his eyes and ears, said Perce it was and shook Pop's hand with a restless rat-trap of wiry fingers.

'Calls for a drink, this,' Pop said and had just started to mix a couple of Red Bulls when his son-in-law Mr Charlton came in. After an evening hanging curtains with Mariette at the new bungalow in the meadow Charley was thirsty too. So, Ma said, was she. Pop consequently found himself mixing about a pint of Red Bull, well-iced, to which Ma added an offering of fresh cheese-straws and a bottle of Worcester sauce.

'Well, what's it all about, Perce?'

'Hear you're in trouble, Sid boy.'

A combination of owl and fox gave Uncle Perce's half-toothless mouth a remarkably impressive twist.

'Oh! that,' Pop said.

'They were chewing it over at The Hare and Hounds when I dropped in on my way over,' Uncle Perce said. 'First I'd heard on it. Why didn't you tell me?'

'Nothing to tell,' Pop said, bland as ever. 'Nothing to it.'

One lid of Uncle Perce's searching eyes dropped like a trap.

'Allus come to Perce when the flag's down,' he said. 'You know that.'

'Who was nattering at the pub?' Ma said, carefully sprinkling Worcester sauce on a length of cheese straw. 'Anybody you know?'

Uncle Perce cast a pair of artful eyes on Ma and said:

'Some I did and some I didn't.'

'Oh?' Ma said. 'Who didn't you?'

'There was a piece there,' Uncle Perce said, 'calling herself Mrs Perigo.'

Ma's bosom, in outrage, was suddenly swollen like a pouter pigeon.

'Don't talk about her! That woman's got no finesse,' she said, pronouncing the word finesse to rhyme with highness. 'She's the one who started it all.'

Uncle Perce went through the startling act of closing both eyes, as if actually thinking, thus looking more artful than ever.

'I've seen that piece somewhere before,' he said. 'And it won't be so long afore I remember where.'

'Sooner I forget her the better,' Pop said. 'Drink up, Perce. You're slow.'

'I'm thinking,' Uncle Perce said, drinking up. 'I'm always a bit slow when I'm thinking.'

'What about you, Charley boy?' Pop said. 'Room for another?'

Charley was readily agreeing that he had room for another when Pop suddenly remembered something. He hadn't set eyes on Charley all day, not since breakfast. Had Charley been egg-hunting or something?

'No, as a matter of fact,' Mr Charlton said, 'I've spent a good deal of the day at the public library.'

'God Almighty,' Pop said, almost exploding over the glass and chromium expanse of the cocktail cabinet. 'Anythink wrong?'

It alarmed him to think that Charley and Mariette might be off hooks again. He could think of no other reasonable excuse for a man spending all day at the public library.

'Better get outside that one quick' he said, handing Charley a large second Red Bull. 'That'll put you right. You look a bit dicky.'

Mr Charlton, looking both calm and healthy, said that there was in fact nothing wrong with him at all. He had merely been doing a little legal research.

In fresh amazement Pop asked Ma if she'd finished with the Worcester sauce for a moment. Ma said she had and passed the bottle, into which Pop dipped a fresh cheese straw. There was no fathoming Charley boy sometimes. Legal research?

'I thought I might get a few tips for you,' Mr Charlton said. 'For the case, I mean.'

Pop, supremely confident that he didn't need any tips, merely laughed in easy fashion, and went on to say that it was very nice of Charley, but –

'You see,' Mr Charlton said, 'it isn't as if you'd done this sort of thing before.'

Pop cheerfully admitted as much, but after all he'd seen it often enough on telly.

'Yes,' Mr Charlton said, 'but you've never been in court –'

'Should think not,' Ma said. 'The idea.'

'Might have been a couple o' times if it hadn't been for me,' Uncle Perce said. 'Remember that time –'

'We don't want to hear it!' Ma said. 'Do you mind?'

Uncle Perce, artfulness momentarily crushed out of him by the second peremptory rising of Ma's pouter bosom, hadn't a syllable to say in answer and merely stared into his glass, thinking.

'The essence of this case,' Mr Charlton said, in a sudden flush of words so professionally assured that Pop wondered if he oughtn't to let Charley boy do the defending after all, 'seems to me this. The case of the prosecution must rest almost entirely on corroborative evidence. Corroborative evidence there must be, otherwise Mrs Jerebohm, as I see it, can stand there until the cows come home.'

What the pipe was corroborative evidence? Pop wanted to know. A bruise or something? Where he'd pinched her?

'That'll have worn off a bit by now,' Ma said, huge body bouncing with laughter.

'Corroborative evidence,' Mr Charlton said, 'is evidence from some person or persons able to substantiate the accusation Mrs Jerebohm is making against you. In other words did anyone else see what happened? For instance Mrs Perigo?'

'She was there all right,' Pop said, 'shrieking at the top of her voice. Calling me an absolute swine.'

'No finesse, that woman,' Ma said. 'No finesse whatever.'

'I shall remember where I've seen that piece in a minute,' Uncle Perce said. 'I shall remember all right.'

'As I see it,' Mr Charlton said in another rush of supremely calm assurance, 'you need call only two witnesses.

124

Mrs Jerebohm and Mrs Perigo, of whom Mrs Perigo is the more important. Alternatively you can elect to go into the box yourself and speak on your own behalf. That, however, I wouldn't advise.'

Temporarily startled, Pop recovered enough to remind himself, as so often before, what a marvellous feller Charley was. You had to hand it to Charley sometimes.

At this point Uncle Perce, dropping an artful eyelid, suggested he might come as a witness too. How about that?

'Why?' Ma said and to this rather cryptic challenge Uncle Perce had no answer except to look immensely thoughtful again.

A moment later a cry from upstairs reminded Ma that little Oscar was awake and with her own calm assurance she left the kitchen to see what she could do for the baby, licking her fingers clean of Worcester sauce as she went, half-wondering if a bit of sauce on a cheese-straw wouldn't help to soothe him down. She hoped Pop wouldn't be put inside. She really did. It would make it rather awkward in many ways.

'Well, I must go too,' Mr Charlton said, 'or Mariette'll be wondering where I am.'

'That's it,' Pop said, terrifically cheerful, 'off to bed.'

'Do you mind?' Mr Charlton said. The April evening, its showers finished, still glowed faintly golden outside. 'I haven't had supper. It's hardly bed-time yet.'

'Then it ought to be,' Pop said smartly and wished Mr Charlton a very good night, with pleasant dreams and all that lark, hoping the urgent hint wouldn't be lost on him.

Alone in the kitchen with an increasingly thoughtful Uncle Perce, Pop suggested another snifter and didn't Perce think the Worcester sauce went well with the straws? Idea of Ma's. Uncle Perce agreed and got outside another snifter in very fast time. This encouraged Pop to mix a fourth and for the next half hour or so they sat drinking in steady contentment, one or other of them occasionally dipping a straw into the bottle of sauce.

Finally Uncle Perce said he ought to be getting back and Pop said he would run him home in the Rolls. Perce, who was boots and odd-job man at a hotel called The Three Swans five or six miles away, had walked over for the exercise but confessed he didn't feel like walking back. The snifters made him sleepy.

In the Rolls he fell into a sudden doze and it was only when the car stopped at the end of the journey that he abruptly sat up, sharply awake, and said with all the old compelling artfulness:

'Sid, I just remembered who that piece is. She's no more Mrs Perigo than I'm the Duke o' Wellington. You're going to want me as a witness after all.'

Driving the Rolls back into the yard, in darkness, Pop couldn't help feeling, on the whole, rather pleased with himself. What with Charley's legal research and all that lark, and now Uncle Perce, things were looking rather more rosy.

These pleasant reflections were shattered, almost as soon as he was out of the car, by a voice.

'Hullo there,' Corinne Perigo said.

'The gate's over there,' Pop said, hardly bothering to look at the hatless, mackintoshed figure leaning against the front wing of the Rolls. 'Or there's a short cut over the fields. It's quicker.'

'Suppose we take the short cut? What I've got to say won't take long.'

'Tell it to the marines.'

'Look, let's not be silly,' she said, 'shall we? Why be silly?'

'Speak for yourself,' Pop said. 'I'm off to have my supper.'

'Listen,' she said. 'Supposing I said I thought the whole thing was a ghastly mistake?'

'Supposing you said the stars were potato crisps?'

'All I wanted to say was this.' Her voice was low and languid in the darkness. 'If you and I could come to terms I might –'

'Terms?'

'Well, an arrangement. Just you and me. Strictly *entre nous* and all that.' Pop heard the dry rustle of the mackintosh as she suddenly swung away from the car and came closer in the darkness. 'After all, what quarrel have we?'

Pop, thinking that so stupid a question didn't require an answer, started to walk away.

'No quarrel at all. All you've got to do is to give me the signal and I think I can persuade Pinkie to call the dogs off.'

'Signal?' Pop paused, half way across the yard. Dogs off? 'What signal?'

'Come back and I'll show you.'

'Good night,' Pop said.

Again he heard the dry rustle of the mackintosh in the darkness.

'After all, it's only a question of pride with her. I don't

believe she really wants to go on with it. After all, who does? Nobody really does, do they?'

'You'd be surprised,' Pop said and a moment later left her standing there, a ruffled bundle alone under the April stars.

9

ALTHOUGH the regular Friday Petty Sessions at the Police Court in Fordington opened at half past ten it was nearly half past twelve before Pop heard a police constable calling his name.

By that time he was feeling decidedly peckish and couldn't help wishing he'd nipped across the road to The Market Arms for a glass of beer and a piece of pork pie or a couple of sandwiches. The court had taken what he thought was a damn long two hours to deal with three straightforward drunks, a speeding motorist, a dustman accused of stealing twenty-three boxes of cigars, and a barrel of a woman, arrayed in a man's cheese-cutter cap, who had hit her next-door neighbour over the head with a coal bucket.

'Call Sidney Charles Larkin.'

Pop, who was wearing a natty black and white check suit with hacking style jacket and a yellow tie, at once stepped briskly forward, said 'That's me!' and stood in the well of the court facing the magistrates' plain mahogany dais at the far end.

That morning five magistrates were sitting and a pretty ripe old lot they looked too, Pop thought. Sir George Bluff-Gore, the chairman, in a dead black suit and plain grey tie, looked more like a dyspeptic pall-bearer than ever and regarded Pop with a cheerless oyster eye. On his left sat a Miss Cathcart, a tall, mannish, peg-like woman wearing *pince-nez*, a thorn-proof suit of nettle-green and a matching hat with a pheasant's feather stuck in the side. Miss Cathcart shared a house with a tiny nervous brown sparrow of a companion named Emily, whom she unmercifully bullied night and day, at the same time devoting much of her time to moral welfare.

On Sir George's right sat Major Sprague, a maroon-faced comatose bull of a man with staring eyes who appeared to be continually searching for something to ram his head against. A Mrs Puffington, a miniature over-neat lady with a shining mother-of-pearl face, sat tucked under the broad flanks of the bull rather like a new-born calf sheltering from the morning's stinging wind. The fifth magistrate was a round soapy bubble of pink flesh named Portman Jones, a retired local preacher, bald as an egg, who quavered at the very end of the bench with an air of impending doom, rather like a pirate's victim quaking at the plank's end.

Pop, already damn certain he wasn't going to get much change out of that crew, presently heard the Clerk of the Court, a tallish man in a charcoal-grey suit, reading out the charge against him.

'Sidney Charles Larkin, you are hereby charged that on the twenty-third day of April of 1959, at Gore Court, you unlawfully and indecently did assault a certain female, namely Phyllis Monica Jerebohm.'

The clerk then proceeded to point out to Pop that he had the choice either of being tried by a jury or of having the case summarily dealt with, to which Pop replied promptly that he would have it dealt with there and then.

'Very well. Do you plead guilty or not guilty?'

'Not guilty o' course. What do *you* think?'

'Never mind the of course. Nor what I think. Are you represented in court?'

'Course I am,' Pop said and waved an airy hand to the little public gallery at the back of the court, where Ma was sitting with Mr Charlton, Mariette, Edith Pilchester, the Brigadier, Angela Snow, and the landlord of The Hare and Hounds. If they weren't representing him nobody was.

'What I mean is this – are you represented by a solicitor?'

'Yes,' Pop said. 'Me.'

'Do you mean by that that you are conducting your own defence?'

'I am.'

'You are quite sure?'

'Sure?' Pop said. 'Course I'm sure.' Moses, for crying out gently.

'Very well.' As the clerk, with a withering look, turned his back on Pop, a solicitor named Barlow bobbed stiffly up and down again in front of Pop like a small tarred cork and said: 'I appear for the prosecution.'

'Defendant conducting his own case?' mumbled Sir George Bluff-Gore.

'Yes, sir.'

'Very well. Proceed.'

A moment later Mr Barlow rose and, in a matter-of-fact tone of voice, proceeded:

'The facts in this case are very simple, sir, and are as follows. On the afternoon of April the twenty-third last Mrs Phyllis Monica Jerebohm, who resides with her husband at Gore Court, was walking alone by the lake in the grounds of the mansion. It was a fine warm afternoon and it was her intention to gather primroses. As she walked along the lake she observed the defendant rowing towards her in a boat –'

Pop, bored already, found himself going off into a dream. He felt ravenous already and wondered what Ma had for lunch today. At any moment his belly would rattle emptily.

It actually did rattle, and quite audibly, a minute or two later, so that Mr Barlow, in the act of finishing his recital of the facts, glared sharply at Pop as if accusing him of manufacturing a deliberately insulting noise.

'I will now call Phyllis Monica Jerebohm,' he said.

'Phyllis Monica Jerebohm!' called a police constable in the passage outside and in the space of a few seconds Pinkie, clearly unable to see very straight, was up in the witness box, grasping the book in her gloved right hand and already starting to read the words of the oath in rapid, nervously simpering scales.

'Remove your glove, please.'

More nervous than ever, Pinkie removed her right glove, keeping the other one on.

Pop, who knew as well as anybody what had happened by the lake, wasn't worried very much by the questions put by the prosecution to Pinkie, who all the time stood clasping the front of the box with both hands, on one of which she still wore a white glove whole holding its pair in the other.

The only time he had occasion to feel in the slightest degree apprehensive was when she was asked if, at any time that afternoon, she had been afraid, and she said Yes, she had been afraid. He hadn't thought of that. She did in fact drop her glove on the floor of the witness box as she answered the question and when she rose again after stooping to pick it up her face was grey.

'Were you in fact more than afraid?'

'I was.'

'Were your reactions in fact those of any decent, respectable woman face to face, alone, with unexpected and undesirable interference from a molesting interloper? – or, for all you knew, an attacker?'

Before Mrs Jerebohm could answer Ma's voice rang out sternly from the back of the court.

'I beg your pardon!' she said. 'I beg your pardon.'

'Silence!' called a policeman and at the same time another policeman heaved himself towards the public gallery.

'Silence my foot,' Ma said.

'Silence in court!'

'Whoever is interrupting from the public gallery will have to be removed,' Sir George Bluff-Gore said, 'if this continues.'

'Come and do it,' Ma said, well under her breath this time, 'it'll need three of you and a crane.'

Sir George, who knew quite well who was interrupting from the gallery but was reluctant to do anything serious about it, simply coughed several times in an important sort of way and said 'Proceed', which Pop presently did by rising to put his first question to Pinkie.

'Mrs Jerebohm –'

He paused abruptly and rather lengthily. You had to stand back and let the dog see the rabbit – that was how they did it on telly. He knew. He'd seen it scores of times. It kept the witness on the hop.

'Mrs Jerebohm,' he said, 'I want to ask you a very simple question. Can you swim?'

The question startled not only the court but Mrs Jerebohm, who almost dropped her glove a second time, and in the public gallery Ma started choking.

'No. I can't.'

'Are you afraid of water, Mrs Jerebohm? I mean,' Pop explained, 'the sort you fall into?'

Several people at the back of the court started laughing, with the result that a police constable shouted 'Silence!' and still another policeman moved on cautious feet towards the gallery.

'I suppose I am.'

'Either you are or you aren't,' Pop said blandly. 'No supposing. In fact I put it to you, Mrs Jerebohm, that you are terrified of water?'

'I wouldn't say exactly terrified.'

Pop, smiling in his cool, perky fashion, wondered if Mrs Jerebohm would mind casting her mind back to the afternoon in question? Weren't almost her first words to him on that day 'I can't swim. I am simply terrified of water'?

'They may have been.'

'Mrs Jerebohm, do you feel you are lucky to be alive today?'

'I suppose we all do,' Pinkie said, her gloved hand clutching hard at the edge of the box. 'It's only natural.'

'Never mind about all of us,' Pop said. 'Do you?'

Pinkie, who had already been more than surprised by several of Pop's questions and couldn't for the life of her see the point of this one, almost inaudibly murmured 'Yes' and then was still more startled to hear Pop say:

'Have you any idea, Mrs Jerebohm, how deep the lake is?'

Mrs Jerebohm, growing more nervous every moment, confessed that she had no idea at all.

'If I told you it was fifteen feet in places, even twenty,' Pop said, 'would it upset you?'

'It possibly would.'

'Give you a bit of a turn like?'

Pinkie simply stared straight in front of her, in silence. No answer was forthcoming and none was necessary. She was clearly having a bit of a turn already.

'Now, Mrs Jerebohm, do you recall that when I rowed you into the bank that afternoon – that's where the lake's fifteen feet deep by the way – I warned you on no account to move until I got the boat moored?'

'You may have done. I was in a great hurry.'

'To go where?' Pop said. 'To the bottom of the drink? Because, strike me, that's where you would have gone if I hadn't grabbed hold of you when I did.'

Pinkie, more pallid than ever, looked suddenly sick.

'I disagree,' she said, after a moment or so, in a remote voice that she hoped sounded dignified, if not calm. 'I could well have looked after myself.'

'Not on your nelly!' Pop said.

'What was that strange expression?' Sir George Bluff-Gore mumbled. 'I didn't catch that.'

'It's an expression,' the clerk said, 'in the current vernacular.'

'I beg your pardon?' Pop said. He had no intention of

being insulted and put so much severity into his voice that the clerk, biting his lip, seemed to recoil visibly.

'Just two more questions,' Pop said. 'What did you do after the alleged attack?'

'I screamed.'

'Why,' Pop said, 'didn't you attack me?'

'Because you were holding both my hands.'

Pop gave the swiftest, perkiest of smiles at the same time only wishing he could telegraph it to Ma and his friends in the gallery.

'So now,' he said, 'I've got three hands, have I?' He held up his hands for all the court to see. 'One to pinch you with and two to hold you with.' Pinkie's face had suddenly gone from extreme grey pallor to boiling crimson. 'Adam and Eve and Pinch Me, eh? Thank you very much, Mrs Jerebohm.'

After the pale and shaking Pinkie the next witness, Mrs Perigo, looked icy, almost arrogant, by contrast. She was wearing a tailor-made tweed suit in a sort of dull rhubarb shade and a close-fitting hat to match.

The questions he wished to put to her, Mr Barlow said, were very simple in themselves but, nevertheless, very important. First, did she see the attack? Secondly, was the nature of it as described by Mrs Jerebohm herself? And thirdly was the reaction of Mrs Jerebohm that of a lady in a state of most alarming and acute distress?

To all three questions Mrs Perigo answered yes, merely adding to the last of her answers that Pinkie was hysterical. This, Pop knew, was the corroborative evidence stuff that Charley had briefed him about and he listened eagerly as the solicitor for the prosecution went on:

136

'One more question. Did the defendant at any time offer, in your presence, any sort of expression of regret or apology for his action?'

'No.'

'None whatever?'

'None whatever. He merely laughed.'

'He merely laughed, you say. Thank you.'

This, Pop knew, was the tricky part of the business and when he finally rose to question Mrs Perigo he stared her straight in the face and opened with a question like a bullet, not bothering to pause for emphasis, as he had done with Pinkie.

'You are Corinne Lancaster Perigo?'

'I am.'

'You're quite sure?'

'Naturally.'

Nothing could have been more haughty than the word naturally and at the back of the court Ma felt her blood starting to boil.

'Absolutely certain?'

'Of course I'm absolutely certain!'

When the fury of the words had died down a bit, Pop went on:

'You say you saw the alleged attack?'

'Certainly.'

'Can you tell the court from what distance?'

'Several yards.'

'Can you tell the court how many yards is several?'

'Oh! three or four. Half a dozen.'

Pop, pulling himself erect, wagged his finger at Mrs Perigo with accusing severity.

'I suggest to you, Madam,' he said, 'that if you had a neck as long as a giraffe's and a fifty-foot extension ladder and a three-inch telescope you couldn't have seen pussy from where you were.'

'Indeed I could. And did.'

Ma, in a fury of her own now, could bear it no longer.

'Wheel her out!' she called.

'Remove that person from the court at once.'

'All right,' Ma said. 'Don't touch me. I'm going. I'll be over at The Market Hotel, Sid. I'll see if they've got some decent steaks for lunch. I forgot to ring the butcher.'

'Good egg!' Pop said. 'See if they've got some smoked salmon too.'

'Right!'

While Ma was being removed from the court, as large as ever but more dignified, the clerk rose stiffly to ask with great acidity if Pop had quite finished with his personal catering arrangements? If so, could the court proceed?

'No more questions,' Pop said.

Mrs Perigo, haughtier and colder than ever, withdrew from the witness box, sweeping across the well of the court on a positive breeze of perfume, leaving the solicitor for the prosecution to rise and say: 'That is the case for the prosecution.'

'Do you wish to call any more witnesses, Larkin?' the clerk said.

'I do,' Pop said. 'Uncle Perce.'

'What was that?' Sir George Bluff-Gore said. 'Uncle who?'

'Call Percival Jethro Larkin!'

138

Quick as a fox, Uncle Perce nipped into court and was already half way through a toothless recitation of the oath before the book had actually been handed up to him.

'Morning, Sid. Cold for the time o' the year.'

'The witness will refrain from making observations,' the clerk said. 'Either about the inclemency of the weather or any other matter.'

'Yessir. Sharp 'un this morning, though.'

'Quiet!'

Uncle Perce was instantly and obediently quiet, though not for long.

'Well, I wouldn't be anybody else, would I?' he said in answer to Pop's question as to whether he was in fact Percival Jethro Larkin?

'And do you at the present time live at The Three Swans hotel at Wealdhurst?'

'That's me.'

'Where you are employed as handyman and boots?'

'That's me.'

'The witness will answer the questions either in the negative or the affirmative,' the clerk said. 'And not by observation.'

'Yessir.'

Pop, before addressing Uncle Perce, again made one of those timely and dramatic pauses he had so often seen enacted, and with such effect, on television.

'I want you to glance round the court. Take your time. Have a good long look.'

'Yessir. Sid, I mean.'

Uncle Perce took an all-embracing, owl-like stare round

the court, at the same time picking one of his few good teeth with a finger-nail.

'Do you see in court,' Pop said, 'anyone known to you as Mrs Perigo?'

'No, that I don't.'

'Quite sure?'

'Sure as I like a nip o' rum on a cold morning.'

'Take a good look at the lady in the dark red costume who sits over there.'

'Her with the red bag on her head?'

That was the one, Pop said. Did he know her as Mrs Perigo? No, Uncle Perce said, he'd be blowed if he did.

'Quite sure?'

'Sure as I like a –'

'Answer yes or no!' the clerk said.

'Yessir.'

'Very well. You don't know her as Mrs Perigo,' Pop said. 'But you do know her?'

'Oh! yes, I know her.'

'Mr Larkin,' the clerk interrupted. 'Can you tell us what all this is designed to show? Where is it meant to lead us?'

'To the truth!' Pop thundered.

'Very well. Proceed.'

'Now,' Pop said, 'can you tell the court when you last saw the lady?'

'About three weeks ago.'

'And can you say,' Pop said, 'where you saw her?'

'In bed.' Uncle Perce spoke with smart emphasis, almost with a snap of his jaws.

'Alone?'

'With a gent.'

Several people in the gallery broke into spontaneous laughter but the various policemen, the clerk, and Sir George Bluff-Gore seemed momentarily mesmerized and offered no word of reprimand. Nor was there any word from Corinne Perigo, who was now as grey and tense as Pinkie still was.

'You say you saw the lady in bed. Can you tell us where this was?'

'At The Three Swans o' course. I took their early morning tea up. One of the maids'd got bronchitis and we were short-handed at the time.'

Pop permitted himself a smile. He was really starting to enjoy himself. The court lark was a drop o' good after all.

'But the lady, you say, is not Mrs Perigo?'

'No. Her name's Lancaster. Mrs George Lancaster.'

A sensational tremor seemed to go through the court and Sir George Bluff-Gore sat forward on the bench by more than a foot, eager for every word.

'Are you quite sure the name is Lancaster?'

'Course I am. I had another dekko at the visitors' register yesterday.'

Pop waved an airy, modestly expansive hand.

'So the lady describing herself in this court, on oath, as Mrs Perigo, did in fact register herself at the hotel as Mrs Lancaster?'

'That's a fact,' Uncle Perce said. 'Yessir.'

'Which amounts to this, does it not' – Pop, television-taught, paused for emphasis again, convinced that this was the right time, if ever, to let the dog see the rabbit – 'that either at the hotel or in this court the lady has been telling a lie?'

'You're right, Sid!' Uncle Perce said. 'And a thundering big 'un too if you ask me.'

'Bingo!' the Brigadier said softly and gave a smile of winning triumph at Angela Snow, who returned it affectionately.

Ten seconds later Pinkie Jerebohm suddenly fell forward in a bumping faint. Corinne Perigo, chalk-faced, rushed from the court as if scalded. Two policemen lifted Pinkie bodily and carried her out through a door, closely followed by a buxom policewoman carrying her handbag and flapping a big white handkerchief. The clerk scratched among his papers rather like a black and white hen searching for a mislaid egg and Sir George Bluff-Gore conferred for some moments with his magisterial colleagues, all of whom looked suddenly like hens too, heads slightly to one side, clucking under their breaths.

From somewhere at the back of the public gallery Mr Jerebohm, breathing like a train on a difficult gradient, pushed with flapping arms past ushers, policemen, solicitors, and clerks and finally disappeared in the direction where Pinkie had gone. In the confusion everybody seemed to have forgotten Pop, who stood not unconfused himself in the well of the court, and it was not until Sir George rapped sharply on the bench in front of him that order was restored. Then a policeman shouted 'Silence!' and Sir George said:

'Mr Barlow, do you feel in the circumstances that you can carry this case any further?'

'No sir,' Barlow said. 'In the circumstances I do not.'

'Very well. The defendant is discharged.'

'You may go,' a police sergeant said to Pop, who went without delay, finding himself two minutes later in the bar of The Market Hotel, where Ma, Mariette, Charley, Montgomery, Miss Pilchester, Angela Snow, the Brigadier, and the landlord of The Hare and Hounds were all waiting, glasses in hands, ready to give him a chorus of acclamation.

'Everybody's staying to lunch here,' Ma said, giving him her own personal greeting in the form of a kiss laid on his lips like a cushion. 'I've got it all fixed. Smoked salmon and steaks for the lot.'

'Well done, Larkin,' the Brigadier said. 'Damn good staff work.'

'Sweet man,' Angela Snow said, kissing him lightly on both cheeks. 'Blistering success. Had 'em cold from the word go.'

'Don't they call it purgatory?' Ma said, laughing splendidly over a Guinness, 'or is it perjury? I never know. By the way, where's Uncle Perce?'

To her almost stupefied surprise Uncle Perce came in a moment later with the old enemy, Mr Barlow, who immediately came up and shook Pop by the hand, told him he had done well, in fact, very well, and what were he and his good lady going to have?

Ma, remembering the word attacker, thought for a moment she'd a good mind to sue him for defamation of character and then abruptly changed her mind and said 'A large Johnnie Walker' instead. That would learn him.

'Yes, you did well, Larkin,' Mr Barlow said. 'Congratulations.'

'Oh?' Ma said. 'You didn't help much, did you?'

'All in the day's work,' Mr Barlow said. 'All got to live.'

'I couldn't bear it,' Edith Pilchester said. 'It was absolutely terrible. Every minute was ghastly.'

'Uncle Perce is the one we got to thank,' Pop said, gratefully accepting a quart of light ale from Mr Barlow, at the same time catching him a fraternal blow in the ribs with his free elbow. 'Thirsty work, our job, eh?'

Mr Barlow laughed, proving to be as human as anyone else after all, and Uncle Perce, finding a brief moment when he could lift his face from his own quart glass of ale, laughed too and said:

'I told you I'd remember that piece, didn't I, Sid? I knew I'd remember. I can see her now in that bed. She'd got a black lace nightgown on – that's what brought it back to me.'

'Don't talk about that woman,' Ma said. 'Don't spoil the party. I always said she'd got no finesse.'

'Well, cheers,' Angela Snow said, her voice more than ever cool and languid. 'It only goes to show.'

Show what? Ma wanted to know.

'The truth,' Angela Snow said, 'of the old Chinese proverb.'

What proverb was that? Pop wanted to know and a second later heard Angela Snow, to the accompaniment of golden peals of laughter, telling him the answer.

'If you're going to be raped,' she said, 'you might as well relax and enjoy it while you can.'

10

IT was not until a warm Saturday evening in early June that Angela Snow, in a pure white swim-suit gleaming as a snail-shell, dived with cool grace from the springboard of the Larkin swimming pool and swam the whole length of the bath under water before finally surfacing and turning on her back to float motionlessly in the sun.

'Pool's christened!' Pop shouted. 'Everybody in!'

Soon everybody was in the water, which shone clear and blue as turquoise. The Brigadier, spidery of leg, his middle covered by what looked like a discarded length of faded pink face flannel, duck-paddled to and fro in the shallow end, where Ma, in a bright magenta bikini that seemed to sit on her body like an arrangement of well-inflated balloons, was playfully teaching little Oscar a gentle stroke or two. Little Oscar, fat as a balloon himself and wearing a startling costume of blue and yellow stripes, wasn't very interested in strokes and spent most of his time bobbing out of the water to lick at an ice-cream, a melting super-bumper in thick layers of chocolate and raspberry.

At the deep end of the pool the twins, together with Victoria, Primrose, Mr Charlton, and Montgomery, were either diving off the board or the edge of the pool. Primrose, grave and bewitching in a bikini of emerald green, sometimes sat on the edge for long periods in a dream, staring mostly at Mr Charlton. She wasn't at all sure she wasn't in love with Mr Charlton, who in turn thought she was growing more and more like Mariette every time he looked at her. Mariette was in the house, occupied with the final touches of preparation to ham and fresh salmon sandwiches, prawn *vol-au-vents*, sausage rolls, asparagus tips, cheese tarts, salads, and things of that sort. She was being helped in the kitchen by a more than usually shy, fussy, and indeterminate Edith Pilchester, who was trying without success to summon enough courage to change into a swim-suit, a royal blue one, which she'd bought specially for the day. She hadn't worn a swim-suit for years.

'You see I'm not all that frightfully good a swimmer,' she was explaining, 'and somehow –'

'Ma isn't either,' Mariette said. 'What's it matter? Go up and change in the bathroom. Pop won't like it if you don't try the pool.'

'You don't think he'll take offence?'

'Not offence exactly,' Mariette said. 'But you know how Pop is. He adores people to enjoy themselves. He's been waiting a long time for today.'

'I know. I absolutely long to. It's just that I –'

It was just that she was so dreadfully shy about that sort of thing, she persisted in explaining several times. She wasn't used to it. She supposed she was getting too old for it or something, she said, and it was not until Mariette finally made the suggestion that what she needed was a little Dutch courage to stimulate her that she allowed herself the luxury of a whisky and said she'd have a stab at it after all.

In the pool, in an evening growing more and more embalmed every moment, the air a pure light gold, Pop was enjoying himself by giving imitations of a porpoise or riding little Oscar on his shoulder. Sometimes he dived under Ma, brushing her body playfully on the way up or down.

The Brigadier, watching this sportive play and listening to the steam-valve of Ma's laughter shrieking into air every time Pop touched her, couldn't help wishing he had the courage to try something of the kind on Angela Snow, but a queer sort of diffidence had come over him too. Every time he watched her white cool figure cutting the water or diving from the board in the evening sunshine he knew he could have done with a little Dutch courage himself.

All this put him into a day-dream of his own and when he finally came out of it some time later it was to see with relief that Pop, in his customary fashion, was handing round drinks on a tray.

'Drink, General? Everybody enjoying themselves? Help yourself. Eats are coming in a moment. Everybody here? Where's Edith? I don't see Edith nowhere.'

'She was in the house helping Mariette a few minutes ago,' Ma said.

'Time she was here,' Pop said. He liked his guests on the spot; he liked a party to go with a bang. You couldn't have people missing when the party was just warming up. 'The grub'll all be gone if she don't soon get here.'

'You'd better go and find her, hadn't you?' Ma said. 'If you don't want her to starve.'

Pop, agreeing that this was something like the right idea, went into the house, deciding to renew the trayful of drinks at the same time.

'Help yourself to another before I go, General,' he said.

The Brigadier didn't hesitate and then, with a drink in either hand, padded on thin white legs to the far side of the pool, where Angela Snow sat gazing at a half-empty glass, softly splashing her long legs in the water.

A palpitating remembrance of all that had happened on the hearth-rug swept through the Brigadier as he sat down beside her and she said:

'Hullo, my lamb. Thought you were never coming to talk to me. Afraid you'd jilted me.'

She was hardly his to jilt, the Brigadier thought. He only wished to God she were. A twinge of loneliness nipped him and then was gone for a moment, banished by the sudden pleasant realization that he was sitting only a bare inch or two from her smooth long limbs.

'How are you, my sweet?' she said. 'You look sort of pensive to me.'

The Brigadier, with a rumbled bark of heartiness that didn't deceive her at all, said that he was actually in fact splendid. Absolutely splendid.

'Sweetie, you're in a dream.'

'Oh?' The Brigadier was greatly startled. 'Really?'

'I've been watching you.'

The sentence was of such direct simplicity that the Brigadier, momentarily unnerved, said:

'Your glass is half empty. Have some of mine – allow me? May I?'

With a hand on the verge of trembling he poured a generous part of his second glass into hers and then added the remainder to what was left of his first. As he did so she felt an inexplicable twinge of her own, a sudden bristling at the nape of her neck, that caught her unprepared. She remembered then how the Brigadier had surprisingly found her weak spot in the darkness and she started wondering what she would do about it if he found it a second time.

'Well, cheers, honey,' she said. She lifted her glass to him, turning on him her pellucid, almost over-large olive eyes. 'Nice, sharing your drink with me. That's made my day.'

The Brigadier, for the first time, found himself looking straight into her eyes. He hadn't realized before how remarkably sympathetic they were. It struck him that they were like wide, warm pools. They held him closely, with a great stillness, and he couldn't get away.

'It's rather made my day too,' he said and to his infinite astonishment she started running one of her fingers along the back of his hand.

Meanwhile, in the house, Pop had searched both kitchen and living-room for Edith Pilchester without success. Mariette had vanished into the garden too and he was about to follow her with a second tray of drinks when an alarming sound, like that of a battering ram, brought him to the base of the stairs.

Edith, in shy haste, bathing cap in hand, had slithered down the full flight of stairs and now lay, a vision of royal blue and purest white, prostrate on her back.

'Oh! I do feel a ghastly fool.'

'All right?' Pop said. 'Not hurt?'

Edith, in her bathing suit, relieved of the encumbrances of tweed, corset, and heavy woollens, was suddenly revealed as having a figure of modestly good proportions. Her legs were smooth and hairless. She had very white, sloping shoulders.

'No, absolutely all right. Absolutely.'

Eager not to miss anything, Pop hastily set down the tray of drinks and helped her to her feet. Edith, clumsy as ever, half jumped, half rolled from the stairs, to find herself a moment later in Pop's arms, held in a palpitating squeeze.

'How's your operation today?' Pop whispered and held her so uncompromisingly close that Edith, who had never been so unashamedly near to anything male in her life, had hardly breath enough left to say:

'I won't put you in court. You know that, don't you?'

'Wouldn't stand a chance if you did,' Pop said, laughing. 'No corroborative evidence. One more?'

'One more. Please.'

Pop kissed her for the last time and a moment or two later, with a final spirited slap from him, she was in the garden, flushed and feeling almost naked as she half-walked, half-ran to the pool.

Pop, following with the drinks, met Primrose coming into the house, graver than usual and with only half a sentence to offer him in answer to his 'Not going to bed? Party's only just begun.'

'Just going to the wood for a walk,' she said dreamily, 'and –'

From her visit to the wood she came back, half an hour later, carrying a bunch of butterfly orchids, like palest green wax insects, which for some reason she gave to Angela Snow, who said 'Sweet. Thanks, my pet,' and then tucked them into the bust of her bathing costume.

The intoxicating, almost too sweet breath of them rose at Angela's throat. The little swarm of greenish flower wings seemed at the same time to give fresh lightness to her splendid bare skin, so that the Brigadier, who had never seen anything remotely like it in his life, suddenly realized that even the most arid moments had magical impulses, the power to bloom sensationally.

He wanted suddenly, in a wild moment, to ask her to marry him, but he either daren't or couldn't frame the words. Instead he started to murmur something about whether she could cook or not, then suddenly felt it was all too obvious and said instead:

'Perhaps you'd come and have dinner with me one night, I mean?'

'Adore it.'

'Which night would suit you?'

'Oh! any night, honey,' she said, saying the words as if she were making a personal sacrifice for him alone.

He could hardly suppress his joy and in a lyrical moment thought of how he would give her scampi, asparagus, and veal cutlets or something of that kind. You could get them all, even the scampi, at the village shop nowadays. It was part of the rural revolution. He would try to cook all the meal himself. He would do his damnedest to make it nice for her.

All of a sudden the tranquillity of the evening was heightened by the sound of church bells. Across the meadows the pealing changes, in practices ready for Sunday, came in waves of crystal clearness, pursued by their own echoes.

'Do you go to church?' she said.

'Very occasionally.'

'Would you come to church with me tomorrow morning?' she said, 'if I came and fetched you? And then come to lunch with us? I've always wanted my father to meet you.'

Almost before his stuttered 'Yes, most kind of you, delighted,' was out of his mouth an ebullient Pop had arrived, loudly uttering reproaches about empty glasses.

'This won't do, General. This won't do. Refills all round, come on!' he said and then to his utter surprise saw that Angela Snow had actually laid two finger-tips on the back of one of the General's hand.

Back with Ma, who was sitting on the edge of the pool holding little Oscar on one enormous knee and a Guinness on the other, Pop confessed that you could knock him down with a feather. It was perfickly stunning. Angela and the General were sitting holding hands.

'Why shouldn't they?' Ma said. 'Perhaps he's going to ask her to marry him. Lucky girl.'

Pop, ignoring whatever slight reproach about matrimony there might have been in Ma's voice, said 'Good egg!' and shouldn't he go over and give 'em a bit of encouragement or something like that?

'Something like what?' Ma said.

'I dunno,' Pop said. 'Like champagne.'

'Give us a chance,' Ma said. 'I'm still on Guinness,' and turned to give a sip to little Oscar, who in fact took several sips and then solemnly wiped his mouth with the back of his hand.

'Let's leave the champagne till it gets dark,' Ma said. 'Why don't you get some fun and games organized? I thought you said we were going to have races?'

Pop, leaving Ma to carry on with the business of filling up glasses, suddenly became more acutely aware of the sound of bells. For some reason they always reminded him of Christmas. They made him think of snow on holly, musical chairs, Paul Jones, and Postman's Knock. They inspired him to fun. And suddenly in a brilliant burst of enthusiasm he was laughing in his most rousing fashion and shouting:

'Everybody in the pool! Going to have Blind Man's Buff in the pool!'

Ma laughed rousingly too. That was a good one. Trust Pop to think of that.

'Who's going to start it?'

Pop was tempted to say Edith, but suddenly realized that he'd better do it himself, so as to hot it up from the start.

'I will,' he said. 'Come on, everybody in. Kids an' all. Angela, Edith. All in. General, where are you?'

Presently everybody was in the pool except, it seemed, Mariette. Somehow this evening Mariette was always missing. Where was Mariette?

'She's gone to fetch Oscar a woollie,' Ma said. 'She'll be back.'

Presently Pop was in the pool, eyes bandaged, playing Blind Man. With one corner of the handkerchief ever so slightly raised he could easily tell the difference between Edith, Ma, and Angela and so knew which of them to chase at the right time. Not that he could miss Ma very well; she took up such an expanse of the pool. Several times Edith shrieked, stumbled in escape and wildly went under but there was a time when he grabbed lusciously at what he thought was Angela Snow, only to find that it was Mr Charlton.

When it was finally Mr Charlton's turn to be Blind Man it was Primrose who allowed herself to get caught. Mr Charlton was exactly the right type for her, she had decided. He was her dream. In the wood she had actually shed a tear or two and now to be caught by Mr Charlton made her confusedly happy. In her joyful confusion, when it was her turn, she immediately caught the Brigadier, who then wandered about the central parts of the pool like a searching spider, desperately hoping it would be Angela he touched. His singular misfortune at running several times into the large bulk of Ma finally made her so sorry for him that suddenly she pushed him flat into Angela's arms and for a suspended second or two he remained there, until Pop shouted in lyrical encouragement:

'Kiss her, man! Kiss her!'

To everybody's astonishment the Brigadier actually did, still with the handkerchief over his eyes, standing in water up to his armpits, half as if at a baptism, half as if embalmed.

The whole thing, so unexpected, made Ma laugh so much that she had to go and rest at the side of the pool. While she was there, choking afresh at the sight of Mr Charlton passing and finally torpedoing Edith Pilchester at the deep end, Pop joined her and said:

'Charley boy's getting fresh tonight. Mariette'll have to watch out. By the way, where is she all this time?'

'I expect she's gone to have a lay-down.'

'Good God. Lay down? What she want to lay down for?'

'She's just resting.'

'Resting? What's she want to rest for? It's only eight o'clock.'

'The doctor says she's got to,' Ma said blandly. 'Anyway for the first month or two.'

In a positive whirlwind of joy Pop raced twice round

the pool before finally jumping in, feet first, at the deep end. As he landed almost on top of Edith Pilchester, blind-folded now, he told himself in a shout that he hoped it would be a girl. Another Mariette. No, he didn't. He hoped it would be twins. He hoped in fact that all his family would one day have twins. He hoped that if Angela and the General ever got married they too would have twins. He hoped even Edith Pilchester would have twins. Why not? He wanted them all, every one of them, to have a life of double richness.

In a second whirl of excitement he grabbed Ma from the side of the pool and ducked her four time in rapid succession, at the same time shouting to Charley:

'Get the champagne, Charley boy. Pink and red! Plenty of ice. It's your night, Charley boy.'

With a thump on the back that almost broke Mr Charl-ton in two he urged Charley boy on his fruitful way to the house and then found himself standing, some moments later, in a sort of delirium of suspense, on the diving board.

For some seconds longer he stood there gazing down at the blue water and all the faces of the people he loved. Across the golden evening the peal of church bells, to-gether with the song of a late blackbird or two and in the near woods a bubbling call of pigeons drifted in on a high chorus of midsummer sounds that exhilarated him like laughter. This was life, he told himself. This was how it ought to be.

A moment later, laughing too, he dived. The evening air flowed past him like silk and from across the meadows came the scent of drying hay.

MORE ABOUT PENGUINS
AND PELICANS

Penguinews, which appears every month, contains details of all the new books issued by Penguins as they are published. From time to time it is supplemented by the *Penguin Stock List* which includes around 5,000 titles.

A specimen copy of *Penguinews* will be sent to you free on request. Please write to Dept EP, Penguin Books Ltd, Harmondsworth, Middlesex, for your copy.

In the U.S.A.: For a complete list of books available from Penguins in the United States write to Dept CS, Penguin Books, 625 Madison Avenue, New York, New York 10022.

In Canada: For a complete list of books available from Penguins in Canada write to Penguin Books Canada Ltd, 2801 John Street, Markham, Ontario L3R 1B4.

H. E. Bates's
Best Selling 'Larkin' Books

THE DARLING BUDS OF MAY

Introducing the Larkins, a family with a place in popular
mythology.

Here they come, in the first of their hilarious rural adventures,
crashing their way through the English countryside in the
wake of Pa, the quick-eyed golden-hearted junk-dealer, and
Ma, with a mouthful of crisps and a laugh like a jelly.

A BREATH OF FRENCH AIR

They're here again – the indestructible Larkins; this time, with
Baby Oscar, the Rolls, and Ma's unmarried passport, they're
off to France. And with H. E. Bates, you may be sure, there's
no French without tears of laughter.

H. E. Bates:
More Best Selling 'Larkin' Books

OH! TO BE IN ENGLAND

Are you taking life too seriously?

What you need is a dose of *Oh! To Be in England* – another splendid thighs-breasts-and-buttercups frolic through the Merrie England of the sixties with the thirsty, happy, lusty, quite uninhibited and now rightly famous junk-dealing family of Larkins.

A LITTLE OF WHAT YOU FANCY

'Mr Candy, the vicar, groping among the raspberry canes, stretched out a hand to steady himself, and instead found it grasping Primrose's smooth naked shoulder. Great God, he thought, how warm the flesh was.'

Things may be going well for Primrose Larkin, but they are far less 'perfick' for Pa Larkin. For in this, the fifth delightful story of the Larkin family, Pa has a mild heart attack. Even though the cunning Ma sends a succession of women up to his bedroom to tempt him back to health, he takes a long time to recover . . .